Beautiful Legacy
Our Roots Run Deep

By
Mindy Lee Hopman

ISBN 978-0-692-78177-7
B New Creations
Betty 'B' Shoopman, Gulf Breeze, FL 32563

Scripture quotations are from the New American Standard Bible (NASB), unless otherwise indicated. Copyright © 1960, 1962, 1963, 1968, 1971, 1972, 1973, 1975, 1977, 1995 by The Lockman Foundation. Used by permission. www.lockman.org. All rights reserved.

Scripture quotations marked (NIV) are from the Holy Bible, New International Version®, NIV®. Copyright © 1973, 1978, 1984, 2011 by Biblica, Inc.™ Used by permission of Zondervan. All rights reserved worldwide. www.zondervan.com The "NIV" and "New International Version" are trademarks registered in the United States Patent and Trademark Office by Biblica, Inc.™

Scripture quotations marked (ESV) are from The Holy Bible, English Standard Version® copyright 2001 by Crossway, a publishing ministry of Good News Publishers. Used by permission. All rights reserved. The "ESV"; and "English Standard Version" are trademarks of Good News Publishers. Used with permission.

Scripture quotations marked (KJV) are from The Authorized (King James) Version. Rights in the Authorized Version in the United Kingdom are vested in the Crown. Reproduced by permission of the Crown's patentee, Cambridge University Press.

Scripture quotations marked (NLT) are from the Holy Bible, New Living Translation, copyright 1996, 2004, 2007 by Tyndale House Foundation. Used by permission of Tyndale House Publishers, Inc., Carol Stream, Illinois 60188. All rights reserved.

Illustrated by Betty 'B' Shoopman
www.bettyshoopman.com

www.mindyhopman.com

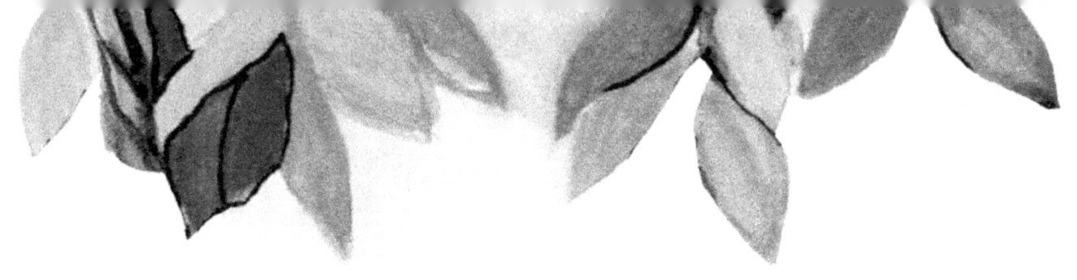

To Jon, the love of my life,

Hunter and Haylee, the children I adore,

and in fond memory of my Jewish grandfather, David Roth,

who showed me the love of God from a very early age

*That their hearts
may be encouraged,
having been knit together
in love, and attaining
to all the wealth
that comes from the
full assurance
of understanding,
resulting in a true knowledge
of God's mystery,
that is, Christ Himself,
in whom are hidden
all the treasures of
wisdom and knowledge*

~ (Colossians 2:2-3).

ACKNOWLEDGEMENTS

When Jon and I established our marriage on the Rock, many people came alongside us to help us figure out what genuine faith looks like in our everyday messy lives. I am grateful to have a moment to thank several of the people who have walked with me through a part of my faith story.

To my husband, Jon, who believes in me and God's calling on my life more than I believe in myself sometimes. Thank you for loving me and for taking the risk of marrying me so many years ago. Every day I am reminded of how "lucky" I am. Your hard work ethic inspires me, but most of all, I adore the way you love our children and show them the Father's love. My eyes well up when I see you lead our son, and how you tenderly speak to our daughter and care for her heart. God lives in you and through you in amazing ways. I respect you and admire you more than words can say.

Hunter, you are the older brother I always wish I had. Thank you for standing up for your sister, guiding her, and loving her. It is evident God is doing a great work in you. Keep your eyes on the prize and let Him lead you. He has a great plan for your life, which involves much more than you can see. It may, or may not, include being on a college lacrosse team, but it will definitely include being on God's team. It is my prayer that you will continue to play hard for Him forever.

Haylee, I was afraid to raise a baby girl because I never liked anything pink or girly, but from the moment you were born, you had my heart. You taught me that it's okay to be tough and girly at the same time, and that's actually a great combination! I loved watching you keep up with your brother outside as he taught you how to play every sport under the sun, and then come inside to play baby-dolls and cook in the kitchen with me. My favorite part about watching you grow is seeing how God reveals Himself to you in the little things. Your heart is HUGE as you always remember who to pray for - every single time. Keep asking hard questions and keep your eyes on Christ. He will lead you through the good times and the hard times. Remember, He is always with you.

Mom, thank you. Sometimes there are no words to express those profound two words. I am grateful for the time and effort you put into raising my sister, my brother, and me. I am grateful we are all grafted into God's forever faith-family tree together. Thank you for your constant encouragement and wisdom. Every time my life felt as though it was falling apart, you reminded me of Who held it all together. You are amazing. *Te amo mucho mamita.*

Tommy and Lauren, your service to God, our country, and to each other is both admirable and commendable. Through the military moves and deployments, God has stretched you and grown you deeper in ways nobody could have imagined. Your walk is an inspiration to many, including myself. Through it all, Z and T are blessed with two amazing parents. Thank you for letting God work through you.

Stacie and Andy, I love your open eyes and wide hearts. God is using you right where you are to pass the legacy of your faith down into the hearts of your three young children. May God continue to give you daily wisdom on how to guide them and love them graciously from His perspective, and may He give you an abundant amount of His strength!

Dale, thank you for taking us to church. Thank you for introducing us to the love of Christ and for being a wonderful Pop Pop to my children. You are loved more than you will ever know.

Cheryl, thank you for raising an amazing son and for stretching me beyond my own limits by giving me opportunities to see God work within my life here, as well as on different continents. I am grateful.

Pastor Robby and Kim Pitt, thank you for guiding Jon and I through pre-marital counseling, and for the warm chocolate chip cookies you served to help us feel comfortable as we discussed hard things, like what it means to be a Christian. Thank you for teaching us the gospel and how to build our marriage on the Rock. Thank you for taking the time with us to plant the imperishable seed. Our lives were forever changed because of God's work through you and your eternal investment in us.

Pastor Jonathan and Debra Winningham, we navigated the waters of marriage, ministry, raising children, and serving students together. Walking with you through some of the most treasured, yet difficult years was transformational and priceless. Thank you for the real, transparent example you set for us as a couple in the church. Jonathan, thank you for looking over *Beautiful Legacy* from a theological perspective. Debra, thank you for being one of my closest confidants. My heart is full.

Jane, my forever friend and mentor, thank you for your prayers for myself and my family, Bible instruction, and guidance. My spirit grew so much while studying with you. I am forever grateful for your prayers and encouragement.

Edwina Patterson, thank you for going ahead of me and sharing your wealth of knowledge. Your wisdom and guidance has truly been a blessing to me!

I am thankful that Kasey Kesselring saw in me the passion and the gifting to take over teaching Character and Community Connection, Old Testament, New Testament and all the other spiritual courses after Pastor Jonathan needed to turn his attention back to full-time ministry. Kasey, thank you for believing in me and for giving me the opportunity to share God's love with students from around the world. Thank you for mentoring Jon and for encouraging me. My heart is filled with gratitude when I think of the support you and Maureen gave to us when we served alongside both of you.

Our sweet Florida church sat right beside our school and grew from eight members to over one hundred when we were there. It was a joy to grow with each couple in our Florida couples small group. Thank you, Mike and Tonya Hamm, for leading the way. We tackled tough topics as God grew our hearts and families together as one.

Today we continue to grow with our pastor Todd Cullen and his encouraging wife, Cynthia. Cynthia, thank you for opening your heart to me in friendship. The support of the women's leaders group, the women's Bible study, and our couples group with Chris and Wendy Sanders has been priceless, especially when I had to leave my children and travel to the other side of the world. I could not have done that without your prayers – His banner over me is love.

Kristen Helseth, biological scientist and eternal friend. Thank you for walking me through the grafting portion of *Beautiful Legacy*. I am grateful for your insight and perspective.

Mom, Debra, Kristen, Britta, and Stephanie, thank you for editing the first version of this story. It has grown so much since then, but you saw it in the raw, beginning stage before I sent it off to the professional editor.

It is true that your editor does become one of your closest friends. I truly cherish the past few months of working with my editor, Amy Hoekstra Seeger. She took my writing to the next level, but I am most grateful for the friendship created through our faith stories, which have now been woven together. I am also grateful for Vicki Prather who spent time proofreading the final draft.

I met my editing team through the writing team at Encouragement Café, a ministry for women founded by Luann Prater. Luann, thank you for the heart you have for women and for letting God use you in amazing ways to bring us together. Encouragement Café is where I also met the incredibly gifted Betty 'B' Shoopman, my illustrator and publisher. Betty illustrated pictures from the mere words on paper and created a beautiful book that will hopefully lead you to the heart of the Father.

To God the Father, the Son, and the Holy Spirit who brings us all together as One … my heart overflows with gratitude.

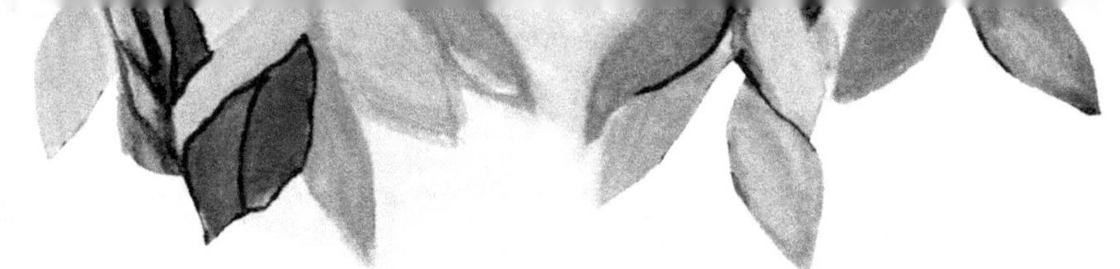

TABLE OF CONTENTS

Beauty on the inside outshines and outlasts
external beauty, because it's eternal.

PREFACE

Since love grows within you, so beauty grows.
Love is the beauty of the soul.
~ Saint Augustine [1]

My husband calls me Beautiful. He called me Beautiful from the moment we first met in high school, and he still calls me by that same name today, even when I am not so lovely. Together we serve and live with our two children on an island off the east coast, where God paints the morning and evening skies in an amazing array of colors.

Even though Jon calls me Beautiful, I struggled all of my life to find the source of true beauty. But through a sweet, two-decade journey, I began to understand the depth of the Father's sacrificial love and the power of the Holy Spirit within me — the source of true splendor.

Beauty on the inside outshines and outlasts external beauty, because it's eternal. This was evident when Moses left his meeting with God from the top of the mountain. His human body could not contain the fullness of God's presence. Moses' face was glowing and shining radiantly! Every moment we spend with God in worship, prayer, or study, He nourishes our hearts, He encourages our souls, and fills us so that we radiantly shine for Him.

In the beginning of our marriage, my Jewish heritage felt like it collided with my intense love for God's Son, and from that moment, I began to seek out the Jewish roots of my Christian faith. At the time, I was both teaching and finishing my master's degree in education with an emphasis on curriculum and instruction. While it was my job to study the scope and sequence of the English curriculum, my training naturally led me to study the scope and sequence of my faith. I was becoming aware of God's presence in my life, when I realized He had been standing by, waiting for me to return to Him. His loving hand had guided me before I even knew it, "We love, because He first loved us" (1 John 4:19).

A desire to know more was birthed. Deep within my soul, I wanted to know more about God's Son.

So I dove into the Word, and I found myself immersed in Him. My life was a sponge. I soaked up as much as I could about the Father, Son, and Holy Spirit. I went back to school to receive a master's degree in religion and Christian leadership from Liberty University, which prepared me for my role as writer, speaker, and teacher in youth and women's ministry.

Fifteen years ago, Jon and I moved to Florida to help strengthen and develop an international boarding and day school. Jon held various administrative positions, I taught wherever I was needed, and our children attended school there from the very beginning of their educational careers. I taught students from second grade to seniors, but my favorite duty occurred every Sunday evening when I was assigned to speak to the boarding student body at Character and Community Connection (CCC - formerly known as Chapel) and to lead the optional Bible study afterwards. Everything in me came alive in that environment.

Teacher and preacher Howard Thurman once said, "Don't ask what the world needs. Ask what makes you come alive, and go do it. Because what the world needs is people who have come alive."[2] A quickening occurs within my spirit every time I read God's Word and know Him more, and whenever I share His Word to make Him known. That is when I come alive. This is why, even though I love teaching English, I speak and write about the Lord in whatever way He leads and opens doors.

Just as I prayed for God to come alive in my own children's hearts, I prayed for and continue to pray for every student of mine.

> Don't ask what the world needs.
> Ask what makes you come alive, and go do it.
> Because what the world needs
> is people who have come alive.
> ~ Howard Thurman[2]

Several years ago, Jon and I felt the Lord calling us away from Florida to a new school in South Carolina. We are thankful for our years of preparation and enjoy continued deep connections from our former school for both our children and for us. We know that our work there will continue to multiply through the efforts of many dear ones with whom we are tied forever through God's faith-family tree.

We are so thankful, getting to serve the Lord where He has clearly placed us for now. At the beginning of every school year, my husband stands before the student body and challenges them with one question: "What will be your legacy?" He asks them to think about what they want to be remembered for when they are gone. He reminds them that their names, their character, and their choices will remain with those left behind — for better or worse.

A legacy is something of utmost importance. Ideally, we have gained a beneficial legacy from our parents or other significant elders in our lives. It is something that we desire to pass down to the next generation for their good. Most people think of a legacy as being something tangible; however, it is my hope that you discover that the greatest legacy you own is the intangible gift of your faith.

As parents, it's our privilege to pass down the beautiful legacy of our faith to our children. But how do we do that? This book is intended to give you a deeper understanding of the roots of your faith, spur your thoughts on how you fit perfectly into your faith, and provide some effective how-to ideas to help you create space for God to move in your everyday life.

As my lasting legacy, I long to help others understand God's Word well enough for them to turn around and share it, so that its power overflows onto others. That is the premise for my online writing ministry, a website called *Basking in His Light*, and that is also where the premise of this book, *Beautiful Legacy: Our Roots Run Deep*, emerged.

My online devotionals and the words of this book are merely arrows I use to point you towards our Heavenly Father. In that same pursuit, I also hope to point you to the living and active words found in the Bible. I urge you along the way to ask the Holy Spirit to illuminate these old truths and breathe life into your study. While I have strived to shine the light on the Bible from perspectives that may be new to you, I hope that this book may not be seen as the end, but merely a beginning. If these studies are not a new beginning, but merely a continuation or deepening of your faith story, then I hope they are a helpful key to unlocking more of the riches and knowledge of His grace.

The more I learn, the more I realize there is so much more to know. But it is my hope that through personal narrative and biblical application presented in this labor of love, you will understand the depth of the Father's love, identify your position in the faith-family tree, and pass down His beautiful legacy to your children and your children's children. ▪

Mindy Lee Hopman

INTRODUCTION
Naches

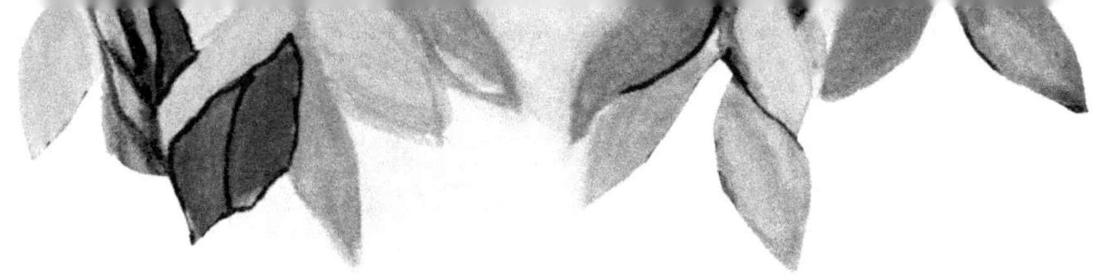

I've learned that people will forget what you said,
people will forget what you did,
but people will never forget how you made them feel.
~ Maya Angelou[1]

My favorite time is summertime, when long days turn into late night swims, and my family anticipates melty, fruit popsicles after every meal! During the summer evenings, my husband and I stealthily paddleboard in the creek to sneak up on our young fisherman. My daughter swims to her heart's delight. We like to reserve our early Saturday mornings for family fishing or tennis matches, where the losers become the scoopers. Ice cream tastes so good when it's served straight to you, the victorious ones, by humbled waiters!

When August turns its sticky corner, the leisurely pace begins to slip away. A hustle-bustle, getting-ready mode steals into my home and tries to take over. My husband begins to spend longer days away to prepare the school facility for the school year; and in the evenings, we join him to help, but really it's so we can continue to stretch out our family time. From finishing projects to assembling new dorm or classroom furniture, we are together getting ready for an exciting new school year. With white knuckles, I hold onto summertime as long as I can, because I know too well how it quickly slips away as busyness invades my soul.

One particular summer, the kids and I were trying our best to squeeze out every drop of the remaining days of freedom. In between crossing off items on the to-do list, I received a phone call from my grandparents. They said they were visiting my aunt and uncle three hours away from where we lived. As I listened to their request to join them, I felt the tension of the crossing-off versus time away playing. My head said no, there was still too much to do to get ready for the fast-approaching school year, but the words from my heart pushed through. I heard myself saying with genuine excitement, "Yes, we will be there tomorrow!" And thus the steady flow of organizing came to an abrupt halt. I left the school books and new colorful school supplies in heaping piles around my house as we packed up the car to prepare for the drive.

We arrived to the hotel in time for lunch and an afternoon swim. I quietly sat beside my grandfather as we watched the kids play. We had always had the best conversations. I could listen to him talk forever about our Jewish roots, from learning about the prayer shawl known as the tallith to talking about rituals done in his childhood home during the Sabbath, like cooking ahead of time, walking to temple, and even pulling out and tearing toilet paper the day before. This day at the pool, he once again enjoyed recounting the beautiful traditions to me.

Suddenly, the conversational flow of words stopped. He looked at my children playing, and then he looked at me. He knew I had dropped everything I was doing to be there. This brief visit, we both knew, was an unexpected gift. At that moment, he looked into my eyes with a tender gaze and he tenderly whispered, *"Naches."* My eyes, big as his, eyes that had been passed from generation to generation to me, reflected the same wonder back to him.

Naches. I did not recognize the Yiddish word. Tears welled in his eyes as he explained. He breathed the words, "Joy ... pure delight." Then he elaborated: When a child brings abundant joy or delight to his or her parents or grandparents, the Yiddish expression for the emotion one feels is *naches.*

Naches, he said, is a deeply emotional word, used when the fullness of the soul overflows beyond the expression of more common words. It was then I realized that sweet joy and pure delight were what he saw when he looked at my children — and me. So it was my turn for my eyes to well up. I looked at him, and all I could say was a whispered thank you. My trip was made. That time-standing-still, love-filled moment made my trip and the interruption in my work more than worth it.

Naches. It struck a chord in me. I knew the feeling my grandfather described. A feeling of sweet joy overwhelms my soul when my son does something helpful for his sister or for a friend, or when my daughter helps my sister with her little ones. Our children warm our hearts when the love they feel deep down in their souls pours out onto others. This feeling of delight is beyond words.

On the way home, I began thinking, "As my children bring me great joy, do I bring joy to the Father? When He looks at me, does His heart swell? Does He feel *naches*?" From deep within, I knew the answer: Our Father in heaven loves us, adores us, and cherishes us. My heart smiled wide as I thought about His joy and how it flows down in abundance to me, straight into the depth of my soul. Then I pondered another, deeper question, "Is my life so full of His love that His joy overflows freely onto others?" The answer came clearly: When my actions reflect my full heart, it must bring Him — the all-powerful Creator of the universe — a father's indescribable joy!

I have spent many years since learning more about the depth of the Father's love through the sacrificial death of His Son. Just knowing my Heavenly Father completely and unconditionally loves me enough to sacrifice His only begotten Son for my sins is often a balm to my weary soul. Do you feel the same way? Does your soul know it well?

When the powerful presence of the Holy Spirit fills the voids in my heart, His love, joy, and peace can't help but well up from within and overflow onto everyone I meet. In the shadow of His wings is where I find refuge from the storms of life and where the faith-filled life begins.

This faith-filled life is a series of holy, conscious choices: loving my husband the way he deserves, cherishing my children right where they are, and being available instead of busy. It's about creating space for God, cleaning up the kitchen, keeping up with the laundry, preparing thoughtful meals, and teaching my children that responsibility begins in the home, because one day they will have their own homes to run. It's about letting go of perfection and holding on tightly to grace.

It's about honoring Him in the workplace by giving 100 percent and loving people from His heavenly perspective. It's about knowing

Him well in order to trust Him completely through the good times and difficult times. Living a faith-filled life is about understanding that my sins were forgiven on the cross and that I may now walk in the Spirit with pure freedom: "Now the Lord is the Spirit, and where the Spirit of the Lord is, there is freedom" (2 Corinthians 3:17 NIV).

*It's about letting go of perfection
and holding on tightly to grace.*

Beloved, you are beautiful because His spiritual legacy runs deep within your soul.

When your heart understands the depth of His love,
you bring the Father *naches.*

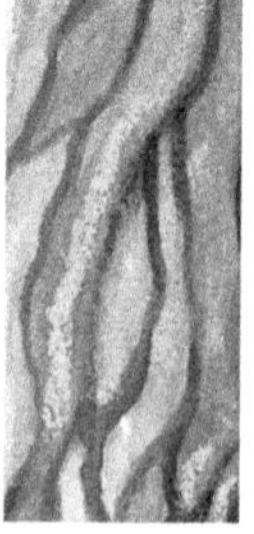

PRAYER AND REFLECTION

Heavenly Father,

I praise You for who You are and for who You made each of us to be. I praise You for Your perfect ways and for creating us with joy for joy. Thank You for helping us understand that you give us the Holy Spirit (whose fruit is joy) the moment we believe in Your Son. The power of the Holy Spirit in me guides and helps me to live a faith-filled life, which brings You joy! May my actions and words reflect the fullness of my heart, so that You receive naches.

May the gift of Your joy continue to radiate from within and overwhelm my soul.

*In Your precious name, Jesus, I pray.
Amen.*

After praying the written prayer, spend additional time in prayer today thanking God for His presence in your life. As you thank Him, some ideas may come to your mind about the ways He shows Himself present. Write those down so you can review and thank Him again and again.

Ways God Has Shown His Presence to Me:

____

____

____

____

____

____

____

Now ask Him to reveal Himself to you during this study. Ask Him to reveal to you a verse to hide within your heart for all the days to come, if He has not already. I call this your "life verse." You may know your life verse immediately, or it may take time to come to you. When it is revealed, write it down in places for you to see it every day.

Write your life verse here:

____

____

____

____

____

____

____

____

____

____

____

____

Hold tightly to your life verse.
Your life verse is a part of your faith legacy.

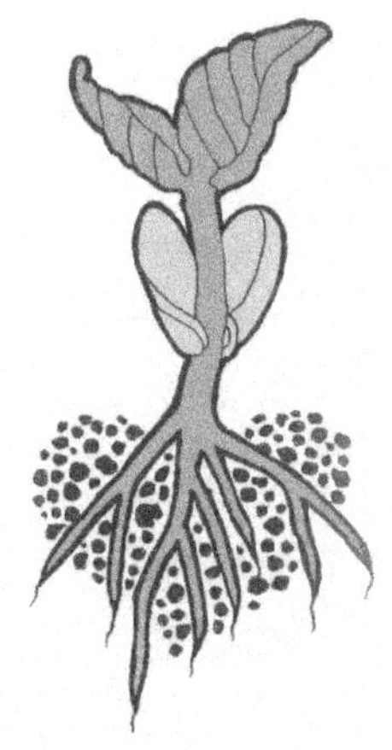

CHAPTER ONE

Created

The question is not what we intended ourselves to be,
but what He intended us to be when He made us.
~ C.S. Lewis[1]

We opened the front door, and the cold blast of wintery air immediately brushed against my cheeks. I stared hard into the dark, but it was pitch black, and there was no one there. I whispered, "Grandpa, why do we open the door for the prophet Elijah?" Why we opened the door puzzled me, because year after year there was never anyone there. "Would this be the night that he actually joins us?" I wondered as I peered outside.

Grandpa explained the beautiful age-old tradition to me, "When we open the door, we remember that God is watching us. God sees us. God protects us. Every year on Passover, we remember how God delivered our people, and we look forward to what is to come. One day Elijah will return."

He told me how Elijah, a great hero of the Jewish faith, encouraged the Hebrew people to make God the center of their lives by turning away from false gods and following the one true God. In the Old Testament, Elijah never died; God swept Elijah away in a flaming chariot.[2] According to Jewish tradition, Elijah is supposed to usher in the Messiah, who will one day come to offer redemption.

Even as a child, from the moment my grandfather opened that door, I knew there was something, or rather someone, missing. The main character of the greatest story had not been revealed to my veiled eyes. I didn't yet understand what it meant to be grafted into the rich and extensive faith-family tree, with God's presence intricately woven throughout history and the promises right into my life.

When God unveiled my eyes as an adult, and I saw His Son as the One who came to save me, the childhood stories miraculously became more clear and real to me than ever. My mind demanded answers to some burning questions: If Jesus was God's Son and He was Jewish, why was He not a part of my Jewish faith? How do my Jewish roots weave into my newfound belief in God's Son, and when did the faith-family tree roots begin? How does my story fit into the greatest story and how do I pass down this beautiful legacy to my children? The answers to these questions were both encouraging and exciting!

I used a wide-angled lens to view the scope of God's love, and I began to understand that my faith began at creation, traveled through my Jewish ancestors, and continues as the legacy that enriches my life today.

In the Beginning

As a new believer, I began searching for answers from the beginning of God's Word, working my way through the Bible. As I forged through, I saw how God uses ordinary people for extraordinary deeds and glorifies Himself through everyday materials (Isaiah 64:8, Romans 9:20-22).

A master artist creates extraordinary art
from ordinary supplies.

This unforgettable truth became apparent to me: *A master artist creates extraordinary art from ordinary supplies.* For example, my daughter loves both visual and performing arts. Whether she is painting, modeling clay, or creating a dance, she fashions things pleasing to the eye. My husband loves to transform wood and nails into amazingly functional and attractive gifts and furniture. My son creates highlight movies from the hours of lacrosse film we take of him, and I love to choose ordinary words to weave together a memorable message. Each one of our crafts uses ordinary materials, yet brings us delight in the creative process, with a sense of satisfaction when we are finished.

Today, if you were given a blank artist's canvas and a palette full of vibrant colors, and you were told to create a painted masterpiece, what would you paint? How much time would you set aside to prepare? Would you begin with the end in mind? Would you decide up front where the painting should go in your house? Would you choose the perfect spot on your wall and pick the perfect colors to complement or contrast with the décor? Your canvas could depict a narrow snapshot of your life or the wide brushstroke of your life's journey. These decisions could influence your final product from the very beginning.

Maybe you are not a creative person, but you love organizing or working with numbers. If you were given a closet to organize or a budget to put together, where would you begin? Would you imagine the finished product and then begin?

The name of the first book of the Bible, Genesis, literally means, "in the beginning." A New Testament Greek word for Jesus is "Logos," which means word. "In the beginning was the Word, and the Word was with God, and the Word was God" (John 1:1). According to Scripture, Jesus, the Word, was with God in the beginning. He was the firstborn of all creation, and by Him all things are created, through Him and for Him, and Jesus holds all things together (Colossians 1:15-16).

In the beginning of time, God designed the world using a specific, intentional order. Since His ways are perfect, His order is perfect as well. Light and dark preceded the sea, sun, moon, and stars. The land was created before the plants so that the seeds had a place to grow in order to provide food for the animals. Once the animals were created, man and woman were strategically placed in the garden to rule over them.

Life was simple — not yet complicated by the schedules, the activities, and the technology which envelop our lives, our time, and our minds today. Adam and Eve maintained the garden, but it was *naches* in their oneness and fellowship with God. Their role in the garden included weeding and tending the plants. This was not laborious work, but a joy for Adam and Eve — just as when we are "working" in our giftedness, we find joy, satisfaction and fulfillment! And there wasn't even any laundry to do!

> Man was created for fellowship with God. God made him in His own image and likeness, so that he would be capable of understanding and enjoying God, entering into His will, and delighting in His glory. ~Andrew Murray, *The Practice of God's Presence* [3]

Oneness

Our love story began when I was fourteen and Jon was sixteen, when we were introduced to one another over a summer break while working together at a small country club on the east coast of the United States. While I grew up in Northern Virginia, Jon grew up on the other side of the world, but we lived in the same hometown when he was stateside.

When Jon's parents were stationed in Sudan, they decided to send him to a private, boarding school in Maryland. While we attended different high schools, we always made it a point to call each other on our shared birthday, September twenty-ninth! Unfortunately, at this point in our lives, we didn't have ears to hear about God's plan for our lives. We were full of our own lives, and we were doing what we thought was right in our own eyes. We fell in love earlier than many couples and didn't know about Godly dating, but God did use the timing and the love between us to bring about His plans for our lives.

*Adam and Eve maintained the garden, but it was **naches** in their oneness and fellowship with God.*

My father left our family when my siblings and I were young, so I was raised in a single-parent, Jewish home. My mother had us keep the major Jewish traditions each year. We attended synagogue when convenient on Saturday mornings, and we visited my grandparents on the High Holy Days of Rosh Hashanah and Yom Kippur. While Jon's family lived in several different countries on the continent of Africa, they attended Catholic mass when it was available.

God was present, yet distant, from both of us during our childhood years. Over time, however, God was calling us both with His invitation: "He who has ears, let him hear" (Matthew 13:9).

In my teenage years, my mom and I were simultaneously dating. She remarried, but that relationship did not last. While she was dating the man who would eventually become my stepfather, I was dating Jon. (Yes, we actually went out on a double date together!) At times, being mom and daughter — yet friends at similar stages in dating relationships — produced tension; however, in spite of that, our family bonds remained tight.

I knew my mom was doing her best, rearing her children on her own. And of course, as I have had a family of my own, I have continued to grow in gratitude for all a parent does, often behind the scenes, unknown and unthanked.

My stepfather took my mom to church where she heard about God's Son for the first time, and her eyes were opened to the greatest story ever told. Like me, she had also always felt as though something, or someone, was missing from the stories about God she grew up learning. When God finally unveiled her eyes, she saw the big picture.

My mom saw how Jesus completes the story from the creation of the world to His arrival, death, and resurrection, to when He comes again. Her beautiful faith heritage was complete when she turned her heart back to God and accepted God's Son as her Savior.

When God redeemed my mom and began to write a new God-story for her life, she couldn't help but want to share it with everyone she knew, beginning with those she loved! Through prayer and by the grace of God, He used her momma heartstrings to pull all three of her children into a relationship with Him.

Our blended family began attending church together, and there we sat — sisters, stepsisters, brothers, stepbrothers, mom, stepdad, and eventually even my father and my new stepmother! Sometimes we took up one or two rows. I remember looking down the row one Sunday morning thinking, "Only God could do this!"

On the top of Old Rag Mountain in Virginia's Shenandoah National Forest, Jon proposed to me at the tender age of 21, and from that moment, I realized I wanted God to be the center of our marriage, but I did not know what that looked like.

The pastor and his wife at the church we were attending with my family established relationships with us individually. I met her for lunch, and we had great talks about family, faith, and forever. She found my family history fascinating. Eventually, the pastor agreed to perform our marriage ceremony if he could be our counselor as we attended a series of premarital counseling visits with him.

During one of our counseling sessions, he asked a life-changing question for us: "How do you plan to raise your children?" We both knew we wanted to raise our children differently from how we were raised. We answered, "We hope to raise our children as Christians, of course."

Very gently, our pastor said to us, "Do you know what that means?" We didn't exactly know how to answer, but God used that incisive question to open my eyes to see His character more clearly. He wanted in on my life, my marriage, and even my parenting. At that pivotal moment, I felt like God wasn't so distant anymore.

Jon responded the same way, realizing the intimacy the Father wanted to have with us. So from the beginning of our marriage, we committed our lives wholeheartedly to Christ, and I thank God to this day that He created a marriage for us that was built on the Rock. Jesus is the rock foundation that holds together any marriage as it weathers the storms of life. I will forever treasure the time our pastor and his wife took to invest in us as a young engaged couple. During that season, our premarital counseling pointed us to Christ, to whom we each chose to commit our lives from that time forward.

From the beginning of our marriage, we held onto the Biblical promise that "the strand of three cords is not easily broken" (Ecclesiastes 4:12 NIV). Instead of two becoming one, our marriage was three becoming one: Christ, Jon, and me. Without Christ, marriage might have been so different. When we wed, we were in the beginning of both our marriage story and our individual faith stories. We were spiritual infants who had a lot to learn about living and walking in oneness with God in our daily lives. We were alive in

Christ, but we also knew from the beginning of our marriage that we needed Him to be our Master Teacher.

The Master Teacher

In the beginning of my teaching career I modeled my teaching style after several mentors. Over time, however, I realized that the greatest mentor I could observe and follow was the One who was a teacher, yet so much more than a teacher: "Take my yoke upon you and learn from me, for I am gentle and humble in heart, and you will find rest for your souls" (Matthew 11:29 NIV). Jesus told his followers He was the teacher, and in Him, they could learn and find perfect rest for their souls.[4]

Wherever Jesus taught, people followed, listened, understood, and learned. People were spiritually hungry, so they listened as He fed them. He knew how to connect and move people's hearts. Jesus always spoke at the perfect times, in the perfect location, and His messages were tailored perfectly for His audience.

Jesus spoke to the people in a way they understood. He used parables, or stories, to explain Biblical truths from a heavenly perspective. To farmers, He spoke about farming.

Some [seed] fell along the path and the birds came and ate it up (Matthew 13:4 NIV).

It's All About the Seed

For the parable of the sower and His seed, Jesus taught from the inside of a boat as the people stood and listened closely to Him. Many of the people in this audience must have been farmers, since He told a parable about a common farming task, sowing seeds. Grabbing their attention by discussing a topic with which they were deeply familiar, Jesus begins His parable with seeds as the topic: "Some [seed] fell along the path and the birds came and ate it up" (Matthew 13:4 NIV).

Here, the seed Jesus referred to was His Word, "the word of the kingdom" (Matthew 13:19). If the seed falls on a hard place, it is unable to be nourished. When someone hears God's Word, but her heart is hard, then the seed just sits on the surface, making it vulnerable to be snatched up quickly. God's Word does not have enough time to be absorbed, understood, and nurtured.

This is what had occurred early on in my life. I believed in God, but didn't understand the greatest story, which involved His Son as the main character. I was even introduced to Jesus when I was sixteen; however, my heart was not ready. It took years to chip away the hardness that surrounded my heart due to events which occurred in my life, compounded with layers of animosity which had been passed down over the centuries to me from my Jewish heritage.

To my Jewish family, even a picture of a cross appeared offensive. During century after century of Christian political and social dominance, and even persecution, many Jews were forced to convert to Christianity and let go of all of their beautiful traditions. This sad aspect of Christian history left my ancestors, down to my modern-day family, with guarded, and even offended, hearts. Unhealed offense like that makes a soul into a hard place. And that offense was

Some [seed] fell on rocky places, where it did not have much soil. It sprang up quickly, because the soil was shallow. But when the sun came up, the plants were scorched, and they withered because they had no root (Matthew 13:5-6 NIV).

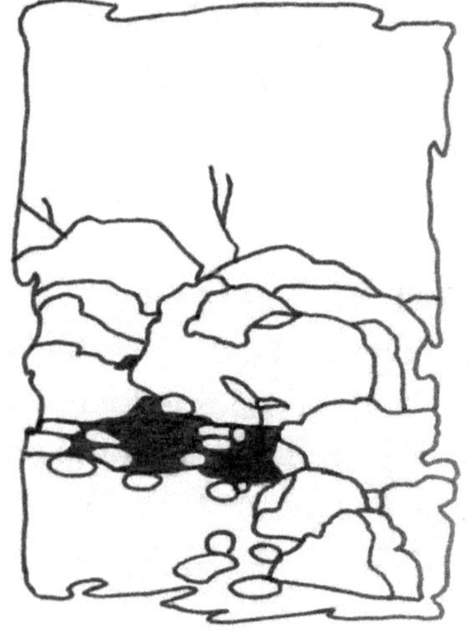

a part of the earthly legacy I had inherited prior to meeting Christ.

In the parable of the sower and the seed, Jesus goes on to describe other conditions of the heart, each of which has described my own heart at different times. I think most of us can relate to the descriptions in this parable at one time or another.

With His audience engaged in rapt attention, Jesus continues, "Some [seed] fell on rocky places, where it did not have much soil. It sprang up quickly, because the soil was shallow. But when the sun came up, the plants were scorched, and they withered because they had no root" (Matthew 13:5-6 NIV).

In this case, Jesus is talking about the person who has received God's Word and is excited about what she hears. Yet when adversity comes, those shallow roots are quickly scorched. This happens because a deep understanding of God's Word has not yet taken place. The roots did not grow deep enough to withstand the heat of a hostile, oppressive culture. This is all too common in today's secular world.

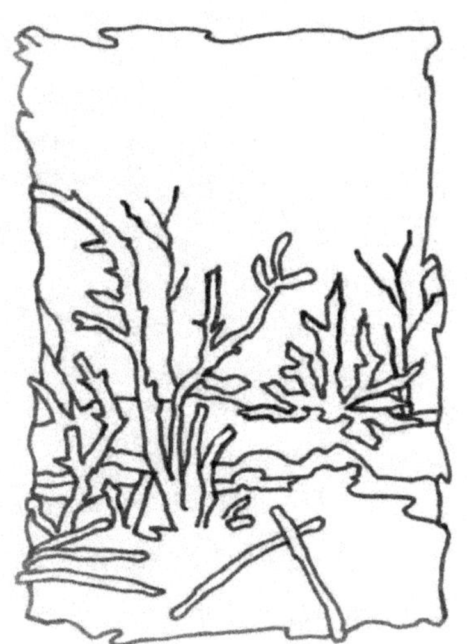

*Other seed fell
among the thorns,
which grew up
and choked
the plants
(Matthew 13:7 NIV).*

I can picture the crowd as they possibly drew in closely to hear what else this master teacher had to say. He explained, "Other seed fell among the thorns, which grew up and choked the plants" (Matthew 13:7 NIV). Thorns, or weeds, in our lives can be family, friends, materialism, greed, or anything that prevents the seed from taking root, growing, and thriving.

When I was 16, I visited a church with a friend. This was the first time I heard "God is love," and those words resonated deep within my soul. I actually understood the message because it was in English instead of Hebrew, and I loved every word of it. I was so excited to learn more about God and His Son!

Then I received a discouraging phone call from a person who meant a lot to me, and I backed away. I will never forget the sting of this person's words, "Some people use Christianity as a crutch." I certainly did not think I needed it as a crutch, nor did I want that person to think that about me. In that instance, the seed in my heart had been crowded out by a hurtful thorn.

One characteristic of thorns is that they prick and bother continually. Thorns are the distractions that keep us from spending time in God's Word. Thorns are family and friends who do not yet understand the fullness of His grace and who tease you for becoming "religious." Thorns are the craziness of our schedules, which keep us from seeing life from His perspective and keep our bodies too exhausted for our souls to thrive. The weight of the world sits heavily on our hearts as we struggle to balance it all.

From the boat, Jesus continues to speak. He captivates the crowd when He shares the good news of hope with them: "Still other seed fell on good soil, where it produced a crop — a hundred, sixty, or thirty times what was sown" (Matthew 13:8 NIV).

Still other seed fell on good soil, where it produced a crop — a hundred, sixty, or thirty times what was sown (Matthew 13:8 NIV).

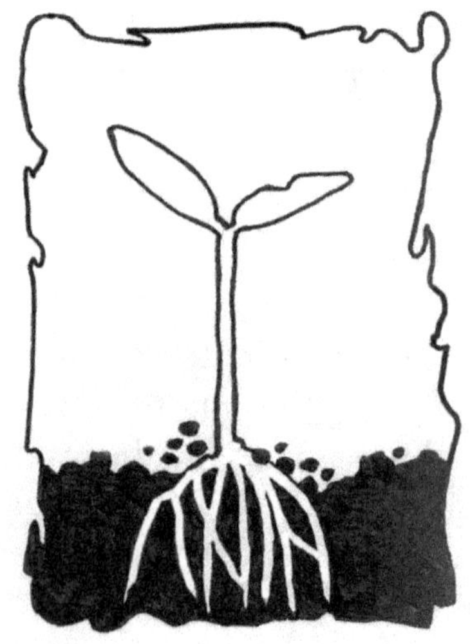

When a person hears God's Word and understands it, it is because her heart is ready. At the beginning of my marriage, I was that person. My heart had been cultivated through the years I was raised in the Jewish faith, and those experiences prepared my heart to receive the seed. When the pastor questioned us about raising our future children, God dropped the seed of His Word into our ready hearts. Jon and I received the seed, and because of it, our lives were grafted into the faith-family tree.

The Olive Tree Metaphor: *The Seed*

The unsightly, rough, and rugged olive tree represents the beautiful legacy of the faith-family tree God planted at the beginning of the world that has been passed down to those who believe.

God offered hope to Adam and Eve embedded in a promise that their seed would one day crush their mortal enemy, Satan. God's spiritual seed carried the promise of hope through a Redeemer and traveled through the roots of His chosen people in order to achieve His plan and purpose in them and through them. A seed produces fruit of its own kind.

It was present in the original Hebrew root and traveled through the tree all the way to my heart and life. Once, I was a questioning Jewish girl; now, the seed sprouted and thrived in a way that uniquely glorifies God through my personal, modern-day story. At the right time, the seed God sowed upon my heart blossomed from a seed fallen upon the ready soil of my soul into a full-fledged, living, growing, spiritual legacy that follows the form of the centuries-old, faith-family tree.

Regardless of where you are, or where you have been, or the different culture you may have come from or your background or past, your heart can choose to be ready for the seed prepared for your unique time and place in history. Created by God, in His image, you can experience the life within the seed of the Word, beginning today. From this day forward, you can forever enjoy the life that comes from being grafted into God's faith-family tree.

What is your heart condition?

Is it hard, rocky, thorny, or is it good and ready?

TREASURE, PRAYER, AND REFLECTION

Scripture Treasure

"… For you have been born again not of seed which is perishable but imperishable, that is, through the living and enduring word of God" (1 Peter 1:23).

Prayer

Heavenly Father,

I praise You for the Word, Jesus, and for Your Holy Spirit. I praise You for their presence with You at the beginning of time. Lord, I praise You for the condition of my heart which You tenderly cultivated through good and not-so-good experiences over the years. I am grateful. Please continue to remove the hardness, the thorns, and the weeds, so that my heart may be cultivated completely. I am grateful that You can see the big picture. You knew You were preparing my heart to receive the seed from the beginning of time.

I'm letting the mess go, and I am ready to receive the seed of Your Word, Jesus. I want to commit to know You more as I study Your generational roots, which have now become my own.

In Your precious name, Jesus, I pray,

Amen

Our faith comes by the saving grace of God, and it is God who grows our faith; however, there are some things that we can do — disciplines — to make ourselves available to God.

Throughout this book you will find a few spiritual disciplines, or habits, to help you walk in His Word daily. According to internationally renowned priest and author, professor and pastor Henri Nouwen, these simple practices will help you "keep time and space open for God."[5]

Quiet time allows your soul to breathe. 

Spiritual Discipline: *Quiet Time*

Quiet time allows your soul to breathe. Your quiet time is a great time to choose to read the Bible. Reading the Bible is not the same as reading the latest fiction novel on the bestseller list. To make it happen, you need to intentionally carve time out of your schedule. A designated quiet time provides time to read and soak in the living and active Word of God. Whether you are picking up the Bible for the first time (which as I know can be scary!), or you feel as though you know every story in the Book, God will give you a fresh washing of the Word if you take the time to still your soul and let His Word speak to you.

Deep Roots Reflection

Your faith journey is the most important story you own. You may not believe your story is beautiful, but the Author of your story has written it in His perfect order, and He is not finished yet. I challenge you to see your story from His perspective instead of your own. As you understand how your story fits perfectly into the greatest story, you will begin to unwrap the gift of the legacy God wants you to pass to your children.

Legacy:
1. a gift of property, especially personal property, as money, by will; a bequest.
2. anything handed down from the past, as from an ancestor or predecessor.[6]

Old Testament Word: *bara* (Hebrew)
to create, shape, form, of heaven and earth and of man[7]

Beloved, it is not an accident that you are here, right now, in the beginning of this Bible study with a heart that's ready. God created you for today. The spiritual seed, passed down since the beginning of time from generation to generation, is ready to take root in your heart, which has been cultivated over the years for today.

Look up the following verses. Write them in the spaces provided and spend some time on the thought-provoking questions.

Genesis 1:27 ~

____

____

____

____

How do you view yourself differently knowing you were created in the image of God?

____

____

____

____

Genesis 2:7 ~

____

____

____

____

God created mankind and breathed His life into us. This breath separates us from all other living creatures. After the world was created, God created mankind to rule over the living things. His perfect order demonstrates His perfect plan. How has God's timing demonstrated His perfect order and plan in your own life?

____

____

____

____

Colossians 1:16-17 ~

____

____

____

____

God created what you can see, and what you cannot see. He created you for today. In what area of your life do you hope He is at work behind the scenes?

____

____

____

____

If God began the greatest story with the end in mind, how does that help you to see the story of your life unfold?

____

____

____

____

Throughout this book, as God reveals Himself to you, my hope is that you will see more clearly the legacy that is passing through you, right into the hearts of your children and those you love, and how that makes a difference in your daily lives.

Faith is not something humans can create. Faith was created by God, is given to us from God, and is grown by God. The Apostle Paul realized that his job was to help people understand the Word of God and help them create space in their everyday lives to find Him:

> I planted, Apollos watered, but God was causing the growth. So then neither the one who plants nor the one who waters is anything, but God who causes the growth (I Corinthians 3:6-7).

Faith begins with a seed that lands on cultivated soil, sprouts, grows roots, and eventually bears fruit. The seed, nurtured by the enduring Word of God, grows in a heart that's ready. Passing down the beautiful legacy of your faith begins with you, my friend, because you can't pass down something that you do not have.

Beautiful Legacy Reminder

The Creator took time to cultivate your heart over the years in order for it to be ready to receive the imperishable seed. Your faith is a beautiful legacy growing within you for you to pass down to your children. As you work out your faith story, let the Master Artist create something extraordinary from something ordinary. God's plans are always incredible – beyond what we can ask or think!

CHAPTER TWO
Beloved

How shall we become lovely? By loving Him who is ever lovely.
~ St. Augustine[1]

God placed conflicts within the next chapter of our story. During those conflicts, Jon and I were forced to lean hard into the Lord. Each obstacle caused our faith to grow deeper in Him as our focus shifted slowly from self to Savior. We moved from our house in Virginia to a tiny apartment in Florida, away from our friends and family, and took a huge pay cut to begin a new, rewarding career serving in a private school. Jon's father passed away before our first child was one year old, and we both continued to try to figure out what a God-centered marriage looked like.

I struggled with letting my husband help me take care of the children. When I was a child my mom played the role of both mother and father in our home. I had to learn how to share the delicate role of parenting. At first it was difficult, but then it was wonderful. God gently guided us in our young marriage relationship as we figured out our oneness in Christ with separate, yet shared responsibilities.

Through church and Bible study, God revealed Himself to us in our everyday messy lives — and we began to see His fingerprints on our past, present, and future. During the difficult events of our early marriage life, and through the guidance of the Holy Spirit, we began to understand that God had all the answers for us.

*God's Word includes stories of imperfect people
trying to figure out their genuine faith
in their everyday messy lives.*

The Bible is not full of perfect people, with perfect faith, serving a perfect God. Instead, God's Word includes stories of imperfect people trying to figure out their genuine faith in their everyday messy lives.

Moses had a huge backstory and personal baggage, but God met him in his hiding and to Moses' surprise, used Moses to deliver the entire Hebrew nation out of bondage. Moses did not know the end of his God-story when God approached him.

God appeared to Moses while Moses was in the wilderness shepherding his father-in-law's flock. Moses noticed a bush that was in flames, but the bush was not burning up. That strange sight caught his attention! Out of the bush, the angel of God told Moses that God had not forgotten His people in their slavery, and that He would send Moses to bring the Israelites out of Egypt as God's ambassador. Revealing His name to Moses, "God said to Moses, 'I AM WHO I AM'; and He said, 'Thus you shall say to the sons of Israel, 'I AM has sent me to you'" (Exodus 3:14).

God called Himself "I AM", or YHWH in Hebrew, as His sacred name to reveal to Moses and the Israelites His self-existence. He was, He is, and He is to come. We learn the same of Jesus in the New Testament. "Jesus Christ is the same yesterday and today and forever" (Hebrews 13:8). Unlike us, God does not need to establish His worth to those He hopes to lead; He is already established. Knowing that the great "I AM" was with him, Moses could overcome His doubts and bravely lead God's people with confidence.

During the time of figuring out our marriage, it's as if God, who shared these words with Moses, was sharing the same ancient Old Testament words with me. He seemed to say, "I AM here with you, and I AM at work, and I have a great work for you to do." At first, my response was just like Moses. "Who me? Who am I?"

We continually try to establish our worth, or our value, in the eyes of those who surround us. We often ask ourselves, "Who am I to carry out God's work?" when what we should be asking ourselves is, "How can I bring You glory in the work You are doing through me today?" When we lack understanding of what it is to be called and sent by the great "I AM," we ask the wrong questions. We focus on ourselves and our limitations.

Each one of us plays a part in God's plan from creation through the cross to eternity. When we understand how we are perfectly positioned in God's plan, we can ask the right questions. We can begin to boldly envision the part He has for us to play.

As Jon and I grew in our knowledge and maturity, God clearly revealed He was working in our lives and that He was writing our brief little storyline that fits within His big God-story. His story encompassed our story. God is always putting together an artful film of priceless images, or snapshots, that tell a profound story. His snapshots of our lives are lovingly planned, sequenced, edited, and inserted into the overall big picture to weave together into His overall design and vision.

Loved

At the end of each day of creation, YHWH observed all that He had made and said, "It is good." That was until He saw that the man He had created was lonely. Then He said, "It is not good for the man to be alone" (Genesis 2:18). Man needed a friend to live his life with, so YHWH created woman out of man's rib.

His story encompassed our story.

The woman was made of a rib out of the side of Adam; not made out of his head to rule over him, nor out of his feet to be trampled upon by him, but out of his side to be equal with him, under his arm to be protected, and near his heart to be beloved. ~ Matthew Henry[2]

Men and women, fashioned differently, yet perfectly, for Him. Male and female, both equally valuable, are made in God's image. We reflect His image as our image is reflected in a mirror. In the beginning that was how He created us — to be beautiful and perfect, like Him, whether male or female.

He took time to design each one of us as His great masterpieces. Ephesians 2:10 says, "For we are God's masterpiece. He has created us anew in Christ Jesus, so we can do the good things he planned for us long ago" (NLT).

Since you are the Designer's masterpiece you are already complete, which means you do not need to change a thing to be perfect in His eyes. When you are insecure or discontent about your appearance, you are not seeing yourself from His perspective. He has intentionally designed you for a unique purpose that only you can fulfill. When you are unhappy with the way you are made, you believe lies. Deception begins with misplaced desire.

> Deception takes place when the outward – that which pleases the eye, interests the mind, or gratifies the taste – takes the place of truth in the inward part, the hidden wisdom in the heart that God gives. ~ Andrew Murray, *The Practice of God's Presence: Humility in the Teaching of Jesus*[3]

Our culture breeds a dark desire that says we must look different or have more in order to be enough. When we are rooted in Christ, we become full and complete in Christ. Yet our culture fights against that truth.

Contentment is hard to find when desire is misplaced. Contentment comes from Christ; however, to remain content with the way God made us, we need to vigilantly guard our hearts and examine the desires that speak to us. Until you eliminate the misplaced desire, you will continue to fight a battle between the flesh and the Spirit.

This has been a personal struggle all of my life. I grew up without Christ, and from a young age, my body image never let me feel like I was enough. Even after I was married for a number of years, I convinced myself that I needed to be more in order to please my husband. I am small in size in all areas of my body, and to many people this may seem to be a blessing, but to me, I just felt like I was never enough. That insecurity gave me so much unnecessary discomfort and trouble.

Let me pause and tell you this: You are God's masterpiece. *He planned for you and created you just as you are.*

It is so easy to buy into the lies and digitally enhanced images of the advertising industry. And our culture has made it common to take medically necessary surgeries to change our bodies in order to please our desires which are rooted in the culture, not Christ. Western media creates a specific image, which we feel we all need to live up to.

I don't need to share the intimate details, because the focus is on the restoration, but just know that if God helped me through my own messy struggle, His love can reach right into your life and restore you too. Through it all I learned that the Holy Spirit will let you go where you want to go if you want it badly enough, but He will not let you stay there. He loves you too much to let you live under deception.

> *Through it all I learned that the Holy Spirit will let you go where you want to go if you want it badly enough, but He will not let you stay there.*

During that unsettling time in my life, God whispered to me, *"If I wanted you to be made differently, I would have created you differently. I created you exactly the way I want you to be in order to bring Me glory amongst the people where I have placed you for 'such a time as this.' Please see yourself from My heavenly perspective. In the areas you feel incomplete, let Me fill you. You are enough because Jesus has completed you. I desire you, and I want you to completely desire Me. I am yours, and you are Mine."*

Whether, like me, you don't feel as though you are enough, or maybe you feel as though you are too much in some areas, we each have a responsibility to seek Christ in our individual circumstances.

In most cases, healthy eating, consistent exercise, and adequate sleep keep us in the place God created us to be.

I clung to God's Word, and I let His Words fill me. I may not measure up to outward standards in this world, or in our fast culture, but when my desire shifts from self to Savior I find that in His tender embrace I am enough.

Is He enough for you?

Does knowing Him give you freedom?

Does it release you to be content in your uniqueness?

You have been fashioned for Him, and you are far more valuable than rubies or jewels. Beloved, you are priceless. God took time to prepare for you and to plan for your beautiful life. Sometimes we may not feel so beautiful - especially when we wake up in the morning! But, just as YHWH created Eve, He created you, too. You are His beloved creation.

God's specific creation continues as each child is conceived, "For You formed my inward parts; You wove me in my mother's womb. I will give thanks to You, for I am fearfully and wonderfully made; wonderful are Your works, and my soul knows it very well" (Psalm 139:13-14). Fearfully and wonderfully made. The psalmist is talking about you! And he's talking about me, too. Does your heart know this?

Does your soul "know it well"?

Does your soul know, deep down inside, without a shadow of a doubt, that you were made in God's image?

It's one thing to read it and understand it in your head, but ...

Can you feel it in your heart?

The Greek definition of the word "identity" means to recognize.[4] Do you recognize yourself from God's perspective? *I created you and every part of you is exactly how I need you to be. Return to Me, lay your burdens down, and I will give you rest.*

God wants to give you a sense of peace in knowing exactly who you are in Him. When your identity shifts from "not enough" to "enough" in Him, contentment fills your soul. This is the peace which transcends all understanding — the peace that comes from a reconciliation of the relationship which was lost in the fall.

God loves you with an unconditional love, and He promises to love you until the end of time because that's who He is. God is loving, caring, compassionate, forgiving, and full of mercy. His attributes always remain the same, and He does not change. He loves you just the way you are. He made you that way. Regardless of where you have been, or what you have done, His love for you never, ever changes. God is love, and love comes from God.

God is love, and love comes from God. 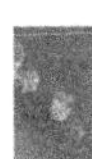

Known

His eyes are on you. They always have been. He knows the number of hairs on your head, the freckles on your face, and the desires of your heart. You matter to Him. He loved you first, and He chose you to bear fruit (1 John 4:19, John 15:16). He was present at the beginning of time. He is present today — here today, right now. He will be present with you tomorrow whether you ask Him to be or not!

YHWH does not notice the flaws we see — the external or internal imperfections. What we see as imperfections, He sees as perfections. YHWH, who made the world in six days and then rested, does not make mistakes. Making mistakes is not in His character. Our culture emphasizes certain traits we think we must have to be complete; but those unrealistic expectations, which we so often place on our bodies or our time, are not from Him.

From the moment of the fall, a fissure, or small fraction, of separation — which eventually became a gaping crack of incompleteness — was planted right in the center of our hearts, making us insecure in who we are. God created the separation for a purpose. No matter how much we do to try to satisfy ourselves, or those we love, we will still feel empty until we let the Creator into the crevices to fill the gap Himself.

In addition to the crevices, our hearts also hurt from wounds. Some of us have more serious wounds than others. Beloved, God knows. He knows when the wounds were received, who dealt the blows, and He knows how to heal them. He also knows if we have wounded another person, because He knows the condition of our hearts. YHWH is all-knowing. He is the God who sees.

God fills the crevices, and the blood of Jesus fills the wounds. Only when we recognize our need for God and allow Him to capture our hearts can we become whole again. Until He fills us, we unendingly crave something bigger than we can see with our natural eyes.

What is the condition of your heart? Does your heart have a desire for personal gain, or do you have a heart that is cultivated and ready to receive God's Word? Instead of going to God first, we often try first on our own to fill the holes with things of the world, like food, friends, social media, exercise, housework, chores, jobs, and other shallow things. But in the end, the world cannot satisfy the critical eye.

A good home: $250,000
A good car: $30,000
A good wardrobe: $1,500
A good hair cut and color: $150
Your heart: Priceless

Beloved, your heart is beautiful, and you are priceless to God.

You are precious in God's eyes — perfectly created for His master plan, and your story fits perfectly into the greatest story.

Are not two sparrows sold for a cent? And yet not one of them will fall to the ground apart from your Father. But the very hairs of your head are all numbered. So do not fear; you are more valuable than many sparrows (Matthew 10:29-31).

Called

Heart cultivation and seed preparation exists in your soul even when you are distant from God. In hindsight, I can see God's fingerprints on my life in many different places, especially when I wasn't paying any attention to Him. My sophomore year in high school, I was listening to a guest speaker who was presenting an encouraging message to the student body in a packed high school gym, and my 16-year-old self clearly saw where I would be one day. Her words reached deep into my soul. The gentle yet firm delivery of her message moved the hearts of the entire audience. She lifted us from where we were, to seeing where He wanted us to be. I was not the same when I left that auditorium. I had sensed God's calling on my life.

God used her to shine His light on me. While I was leaning in and listening, I heard God say, "You will speak to many." As the speaker delivered her message, I unmistakably heard my calling, and from that day, I knew I would eventually have the opportunity to speak and encourage others like she did. I had no clue how it would happen. One does not exactly wake up and become a well-versed, motivational teacher or preacher. There is a process one goes through by serving to get to the point of leading, which is actually the pinnacle of serving.

There is a process one goes through by serving to get to the point of leading, which is actually the pinnacle of serving.

At the time, I was a tiny, shy, young Jewish girl, raised in a single-parent home, who possessed no self-confidence. God was continuing to cultivate my heart. His work of soul-seed preparation traced back to the beginning of time. He had initiated the loving process of drawing my husband and me, and eventually our children, to Himself. God calls each one of us to Himself in His perfect timing and helps us to recognize ourselves in Him.

The soul, in the preceding degrees, loves and is loved in return; she seeks and she is sought; she calls and is called. But in this, in an admirable and ineffable way, she lifts and is lifted up; she holds and is herself held; she clasps and she is closely embraced, and by the bond of love she unites herself to God, one with one, alone with Him.
~ St. Thomas Aquinas, *The Graces of Interior Prayer*[5]

You are His beloved from the beginning of time. He knows you. God chose you. While He has been patiently waiting for you, it's your choice to choose to walk with Him today. Will you let the Creator in to fill the crevices of your heart? Will you let Him make you whole again? In order to walk closer to Him, what do you need to let go of? Where do you need His forgiveness? His grace is waiting for you.

Singer/songwriter Christy Nockels wrote about God's patience with His children as they slowly learn to rely on Him in her song titled "For Your Splendor." The lyrics of this song spoke volumes to me the first time I heard it and used it for worship while teaching *Beautiful Legacy*. It speaks of the perspective shift God hopes we will obtain when the deep seed takes up residence in our hearts, and we realize that our roots run deep in Him.

The Olive Tree Metaphor: *Rooted*

Thick and massive roots run deep and wide from the base of the olive tree. The imperishable seed, represented by Jesus and birthed as a result of our belief in Him, grew roots and then traveled through the lives of the patriarchs — from Adam to Noah, then to Abraham, Isaac, and Jacob. When the seed sprouted up, it created the ancient Hebrew root (the stock or original tree), and displayed the beginning of the greatest story.

The roots of the olive tree carry the covenants created by God to His people over the test of time. In the roots of our faith we, "understand that the universe was formed at God's command, so that what is seen was not made out of what was visible" (Hebrews 11:3 NIV).

In the roots of our faith, we see that throughout time, God could have destroyed the original tree many times because of the never-

For Your Splendor

I'm so concerned with what I look like from the outside
And will I blossom into what You hope I'll be
Yet You're so patient just to help me see
The blooms come from a deeper seed
That You planted in me

Sometimes it's hard to grow
When everybody's watching
To have your heart pruned by the One
Who knows best
And though I'm bare and cold
I know my season's coming
And I'll spring up in Your endless faithfulness

With my roots deep in You
I'll grow the branch that bears the fruit
And though I'm small I'll still be standing in the storm.
Cause I am planted by the river
By Your streams of living water
And I'll grow up strong and beautiful
All for Your splendor Lord

So with my arms stretched out
I'm swaying to Your heartbeat
I'm growing with the sound of Your voice calling
You're bringing out the beauty that You have put in me
For Your joy and for Your glory falling, oh

Raise me in Your love, love, love, You raise me in Your love
Raise me in Your power. Thank You, thank You Lord

ending cycle of mankind's heart: follow, rebel, repent, and then follow again. Regardless of how much we love God, our human hearts tend to go our own ways, unless we rely on our faith.

In the roots of our faith, we see that Noah built a large boat to save his family from the flood, "By faith Noah, when warned about things not yet seen, in holy fear built an ark to save his family. By his faith he condemned the world and became heir of the righteousness that is in keeping with faith" (Hebrews 11:7 NIV). God blessed Noah and created a covenant with Him when He promised He would never again destroy the world by water (Genesis 9:11). Whenever we see a bow in the sky, we are reminded of God's unconditional promise to us through Noah.

In the roots of our faith we see that, "By faith Abraham, when called to go to a place he would later receive as his inheritance, obeyed and went, even though he did not know where he was going" (Hebrews 11:8 NIV). In the scriptural record of our roots, we see that God blessed Abraham. God created a covenant with Abraham when He told him that He would make Abraham's descendants as numerous as the stars in the sky (Genesis 15:5), give them a land to live on (Genesis 15:7), and be their God (Genesis 17:8). The sign of Abraham's covenant was circumcision (Genesis 17:11).

 *When man does not recognize himself in God, the creation tends to stray from the Creator.*

In the roots of our faith, we see how belief shaped our ancestors who have gone before us as our belief shapes our lives today. The moment you believe in God, He adopts you as His child and places your name within the greatest story, intricately woven in the likeness of a faith-family tree, where the ancient roots travel all the way back to the beginning of time.

And thus, our identity changes when we become a child of God. When we recognize ourselves in God, we understand that we are complete, rooted, and grounded in God. When we fail to find our identity in God, we stray from His plan for our lives. *When man does not recognize himself in God, the creation tends to stray from the Creator.* Like the olive tree, our soul's new roots are thick and massive, running both deep and wide, keeping us steady and giving us a fixed anchor for the wavering soul.

Thanks to the stability and depth of the root system, the faith-family tree flourished and demonstrated God's love, an everlasting love, which gives mankind the beautiful, merciful opportunity in which to be grafted.

TREASURE, PRAYER, AND REFLECTION

Scripture Treasure

"For we are God's masterpiece. He has created us anew in Christ Jesus, so we can do the good things he planned for us long ago" (Ephesians 2:10 NLT).

Heavenly Father,

I praise You for making me in Your image. Since You are worthy, and I am Your creation, that makes me loved and priceless. I am grateful for the opportunity to be known by You and to know You. I am grateful that You loved me first. Thank You for calling me into Your holy presence, so that I may learn about You, grow, and love others.

In Your precious name, Jesus, I pray,
Amen

Spiritual Discipline: *Prayer*

Prayer may happen silently or out loud. When you pray, you are talking to your Father in heaven. He loves you just as you are. Prayer is similar to a letter to God which usually includes an introduction, a body, and a conclusion.

Here's your assignment for this chapter: Pray silently or out loud for 30 seconds, or more if you want to. Pray for God to reveal Himself to you throughout this study. Pray for answers to the application questions which have been written to reveal God to you and help you work out your faith. When your prayer comes from your heart, it does not have to be fancy, just faithful. Remember, God created you for fellowship with Him. You were made for this.

Deep Roots Reflection
Old Testament Word: *hesed* (Hebrew)
goodness, kindness, faithfulness[7]

Hesed love is everlasting and faithful. It represents deep, unconditional love that comes from years of marriage, or is given from a parent to a child. It's watching an elderly couple laugh at their own jokes from years of understanding, or accepting a child back into your home even after he or she has disappointed you. Hesed love is not Valentine's Day, romantic, pink, and fluffy love. Instead, it's everlasting love, which offers mercy and grace to those who choose to accept it. Hesed love is not based on feelings, but rather, on actions.

This feast of God's Word has been carefully prepared for your heart. It comes with a full helping of grace, mercy, and hesed for your heart. The following questions will help you to work out your faith and understand the legacy you own, so that you may pass it down to your children.

Look up the following verses and write them in the spaces provided. Then take time to answer the following questions:

Isaiah 54:10 ~

____

____

____

____

____

God's lovingkindness will never be removed from you. How does this verse change your actions or your outlook on your life?

____

____

____

____

____

1 Peter 2:9-10 ~

____

____

____

____

You are His chosen people. He has moved you from darkness to light. When did this happen in your life?

____

____

____

____

God sees the big picture from the beginning of time to the end of time, and He sees exactly where you fit into it.

God is omnipotent. He is all-powerful. God breathed the stars into existence. He is the Master Designer. Where have you seen the power of God's love in your life? Write about one situation He has brought you through. How did this situation change your life, or your outlook for the better?

____

____

____

____

God is omniscient. He is all-knowing. How well do you think you know your spouse, or a close friend? How well do you know your children? Do you know how many hairs any of them have on their heads? How does it feel to realize that God knows the answers to these questions, and He even knows the condition of our hearts? How can you keep your heart in suitable condition for His Word to land on?

____

____

____

____

What are your favorite traits? Are you funny? Friendly? Caring? Compassionate? Athletic? Let your favorite traits resonate in your heart for a little while. They are a part of who God created you to be. He meant for you to enjoy them. Not only were you made to His perfection and for His glory, but you also matter to Him.

____

____

____

____

____

____

God is omnipresent. It does not matter how hard you try to hide, because you cannot hide from Him. He is always with you. When do you sense His presence the most? Have you taken time this week to spend with Him? It's never too late to begin today. When you were still for just a few moments in the presence of the Creator, what did you notice?

____

____

____

____

____

____

God is always there for you, just as you try to be for your own children. Social media, the phone, and texting do not distract God. You have His complete and undivided attention, 100 percent of the time. Do your children feel the same way about you? What would they say if a friend of yours asked them that question? Would they say you are attentive toward them, or would they say you are always on your phone or on your computer? Remember, we are setting examples for our children.

Let me affirm something: You will never regret setting aside time for your family. We cannot multi-task like God the Father can, or be present at all times like He is, but making the effort to follow His perfect parenting example is always worth the sacrifice.

The first part of your calling is to commit yourself to Christ. This is the most vital part of your faith story. Some people will say the most important decision in your life is choosing whom you will marry. I agree that the decision of whom to marry is very important, but even more important — in fact, the most vital decision you will make on your own — is to accept God's Son or reject Him.

If you choose to accept His invitation to come into a relationship with Him, here is a simple prayer to pray (you may say it anywhere):

Heavenly Father,

Thank You for loving me first, even in my everyday mess. Thank You for sending Your Son as a sacrifice for my sins yesterday, today, and tomorrow. I believe in Him and commit my life to Him from this day forward.

In Your precious name, Jesus, I pray,
Amen

You may ask, "Once I commit myself to God, how do I know His call on my life?" Your answer stems from the mission of every believer: to know Him and make Him known.

Three questions may help to clarify the call of God.

Have I made up my mind to do what He says, no matter the cost? Am I faithfully reading His Word and praying? Am I obedient in what I know today of His will?
~ Elisabeth Elliot, *Keep a Quiet Heart* [8]

Complete the following statement:

In my heart, I know God has called me to:

____

____

____

____

_________________________________.

You cannot have a wrong answer. Your calling may be to be a spouse, a parent, or to remain single. Or maybe your calling is into a certain career. God may be calling you to be a missionary — or a project manager! Whatever your calling is, it's unique to you because God placed a desire for it in your heart. Stepping-stones, placed throughout your life, have brought you to where you are today.

It is the nature of love to transform the lover into the object loved. ~ St. Thomas Aquinas [9]

Beautiful Legacy Reminder

You are God's beloved masterpiece. The Father who has adopted you into His forever family loves you. He knows you, and He will continue to place stepping stones in your life in order to lead you exactly where He wants you to be – one stepping stone at a time. God has prepared you for where you are today, and He is preparing you for where you will be tomorrow. He was always present throughout your life, and He is always present today.

*For we are
God's masterpiece.
He has created us anew
in Christ Jesus,
so we can do
the good things
he planned for us
long ago*

~ (Ephesians 2:10 NLT).

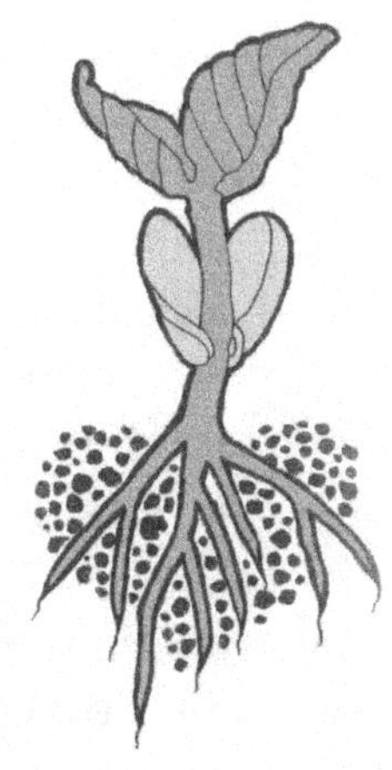

CHAPTER THREE

Curious

*When the eyes of the soul looking out
meet the eyes of God looking in,
heaven has begun right here on earth.*
~ A.W. Tozer [1]

The scar tissue stretches wide across my son's left pointer finger. Whenever my eye catches Hunter's hand, I am reminded of when he was only one year old, and I had the iron out while I was packing my clothes to go visit my family. I didn't even realize that my curious son, who was playing with his trucks nearby, had been carefully watching me. We both left the bedroom so I could get dinner started, but as soon as I turned my back, he quietly returned to my bedroom, where he climbed into a chair, stood beside the ironing board, and pretended to iron just like his mommy. Unfortunately, he decided the wrinkles in his tiny fingers needed ironing, resulting in two very bad burns and lots of scar tissue.

These are not his only scars; he also has some deep ones on his face from a dog attack that happened just before his sister was born, and other various ones on his active teenage body, and I'm sure there are more to come. He has gathered quite a collection of battle wounds from playing rough outside and inside. Each scar on his body tells a part of his story while visually displaying a different unforgettable experience. Each scar is a part of who he is.

We teach our children the word *no* from the age they can reach the danger, but there is something inside of them that raises their sense of curiosity from the moment that enticing word *no* is spoken. Our curiosity can cause both external and/or internal battle wounds. We all have them. Some wounds were inflicted upon us; however, others we inflicted upon ourselves.

Children learn that *if* they do this, *then* this will happen. By teaching rules, or boundaries, authority figures are usually trying to help avoid injury or bad consequences.

Unfortunately, boundaries, created out of love and put into place for our safety and protection, may at first appear as meaningless rules to many of us. Some people, the natural rule followers, accept and respect boundaries for exactly what they are. However, the natural rule breakers go for the thrill of getting up close to the boundary, crossing over it quickly, or just curiously sticking their toe in to test the waters.

Curiosity is a positive character trait that many successful people possess. Having a sense of curiosity means that we care. We want to know how things work in order to see beyond our current understanding. It was curiosity that took us away from God, and it is curiosity that leads us back to Him.

When curiosity is taken too far, it may lead us outside of His safe boundaries. Broken boundaries lead to consequences. If not for consequences, why would a child, or even an adult, stay within the boundaries which don't seem logical? As my teenage son learns to drive, I encourage him to follow the speed limit out of the fear that he might lose control, or not be able to react quickly enough should someone pull out in front of him. The speed limit is set for his own safety and protection. If he would break the speed limit boundary, the consequence could be a ticket, hopefully not something much worse.

God, the perfect Father, says that His discipline stems from His love for us. He says in Revelation 3:19, "Those whom I love, I reprove and discipline." Raising children well requires an intentional sense of physical and spiritual discipline.

The Apostle Paul, who was called to share the gospel, understood the importance of passing down the legacy of our faith to the adults and then to the children. He said in his letter to the Ephesians, "Fathers, do not provoke your children to anger, but bring them up in the discipline and instruction of the Lord" (Ephesians 6:4).

The Greek word used in the New Testament for discipline — *paideuó*— means to train children, to educate, and to mold character.[2] The concept of *paideuó* includes the whole training and education of the child, including caring for the body, correcting mistakes, curbing passions, and cultivating the soul. It involves teaching virtue as it appears in every aspect of one's life.

The Ultimate Creation

God lives in and loves community. The first community contained the Father, Son, and Holy Spirit. After the creation of the world, the final, ultimate creation was Adam. Even though Adam enjoyed unhindered relationship with God, God decided that Adam needed a companion. God said, "It is not good for the man to be alone; I will make him a helper suitable for him" (Genesis 2:18). And so God created Eve. Woman, God's crowning masterpiece, would be the perfect complement to the male creation. We fit perfectly together and since we were designed in His image, we, like our first ancestors, were made to live life together, in community, with Him.

Perfection permeated the Garden of Eden. God's presence allowed for Adam and Eve to live in freedom with oneness in Him. Dew came from the ground to water the plants. Food was abundant. Adam and Eve could go anywhere they wanted. They enjoyed access to every blessing in the garden — the food, the peace, and, above all, face-to-face communion with God.

If the Father, Son, and Holy Spirit lived in perfect fellowship with man in the beginning of time, why do we not live together now?

When did the separation occur?

Why do we spend our lives trying to get back to Him to live as one?

At the root of every conflict there is always a backstory.

The Backstory

Only when you understand the backstory of pride, can your heart obtain the peace that transcends all understanding. Each one of us contends with pride; however, our hearts are not where pride began. The backstory of pride began in heaven when the all knowing and all powerful YHWH banished Lucifer, an angel otherwise known as Satan, from heaven, "This great dragon — the ancient serpent called the devil, or Satan, the one deceiving the whole world — was thrown down to the earth with all his angels" (Revelation 12:9 NLT).

God banished Lucifer with his angels from heaven, because sinless and perfect YHWH cannot tolerate the sin of pride in His presence. When Lucifer became God's adversary, He also became yours.

God always gives us an opportunity to choose.

The Freedom to Choose

Here is the good news, God always gives us an opportunity to choose. God gifted Adam and Eve, and all of mankind, with what we call free will. He did not want His people to merely possess automatic, or forced, devotion towards Him. Instead, He wanted chosen devotion resulting from a complete understanding of the love relationship between the Father and His children.

Forcing someone to do something unwanted causes rebellion and strife. A child loves his or her parent because of who he or she is, regardless of whether or not he or she is a good parent. Even though my father was not present very often in my life as I was growing up, I always loved him because he was my father. In the same way, God loved us from the moment He created us. He hopes we choose to love Him; however, the freedom to choose may also lead us in an opposing direction. Just as in children, sometimes pride enters our hearts when we, the created, think we are equal to the Creator.

Pride is thinking that boundaries do not apply to us, and pride produces pain, insecurity, and separation from God. It says I don't need God, I make my own decisions. Pride puts our focus on ourselves and takes it off of our Savior.

The Adversary's Schemes

Our adversary is a schemer. Second Corinthians 11:14 leaves no doubt that "Satan disguises himself as an angel of light." Peter also warns New Testament believers "Stay alert! Watch out for your great enemy, the devil. He prowls around like a roaring lion, looking for someone to devour" (1 Peter 5:8 NLT). Satan planned the exact words he would use to penetrate Eve's heart in order to slyly lead her to temptation.

*Pride puts our focus on ourselves
and takes it off of our Savior.*

At this point in the story, pride entered the picture and the familiar pattern emerged. Eve told the serpent what the Father had told Adam, that if they ate the fruit from the tree in the middle of the Garden of Eden, then they would die. The death God warned us about was not a physical death, but rather a spiritual death.

Just as the sin of pride caused the angel Lucifer to fall, the sin of pride caused the fall of Adam and Eve from the Garden of Eden. Curiosity got the best of them, and they didn't even see it coming! Satan told Eve that if she would eat the fruit then she would be like God (Genesis 3:4-5). Eve believed Satan's deceptive lie when her thinking shifted from avoiding the forbidden fruit (which was the only boundary God gave to Adam and Eve) to imagining the fruit would be good for food and wisdom. Eve wanted to be wise like God. She was curious about what that would be like, so she ate the fruit and shared it with her husband (Genesis 3:6). It was a team effort. They chose to eat the forbidden fruit.

Even today, the deceiver tries to convince us of lies that are not true. The battle for our souls continues in our lives every day. As a father's heart grieves when his children disobey him, YHWH's heart must grieve when His children choose pride. As parents, grandparents, or close friends, when those we love choose to live differently from our instruction, our hearts break — so must the Father's.

Nakedness Covered

After they ate the fruit, Adam and Eve saw each other naked for the very first time. They hid from the One who loved their souls. By name, He called out, "Where are you?" (Genesis 3:7-13). Do you really think God didn't know? Remember, God is omnipresent and omniscient. He is always there, and He knows all (Psalm 139: 7-12). He knew, but He was searching their hearts. He wanted them to tell Him.

A loving father molds and disciples
his children into the people
he wants them to become when they grow up.

Curiosity drives us near, but accountability pushes us away from God. As humans, we do not like to take responsibility for our own actions when they are not good. There is something deep within our human nature that causes us to flee from accountability.

God, the perfectly good Parent, had no choice but to follow through. In essence, He had already said, *"If you do this, then this will happen."* A loving father molds and disciples his children into the people he wants them to become when they grow up. God the Father had to keep His word and follow through. Their sin fractured and shattered their souls.[3]

Even though they messed up, God still loved them. When they were caught, their eyes were wide open. Adam and Eve realized the depth of God's love, and they repented (or turned back to Him and asked Him for forgiveness). Then God helped Adam and Eve understand that the ultimate deceiver had deceived them. God offered forgiveness; however, consequences always follow poor choices. Through Adam and Eve, sin entered the world: "Therefore, just as through one man sin entered into the world, and death through sin, and so death spread to all men, because all sinned" (Romans 5:12).

God keeps His promises. He does not change. When my young son or daughter apologizes for playing in the road, it's easy for me to forgive their sweet, repentant hearts because of how much I love them. But if I forgave them for making the choice, but did not offer a consequence, who is to say that they would not choose to make that same choice again?

The responsibility of being a parent is the greatest, yet most difficult job in the world. As God forgives us, we must learn to forgive. Following through with a consequence for the behavior helps us to remember not to make that same choice again. God always follows through. Adam and Eve, as the first humans, represented all of mankind. The consequence for Adam and Eve's choice is now a broken relationship between the Father and mankind. Genesis 3:23 says that The LORD God banished them from the garden of Eden in order to work the ground from which they had been made.

Oneness with God, which was present in Eden, was lost. They knew they were naked. So God gave them clothes made of animal skins, and that was the beginning of the laundry pile!

God took a life in order to give life. According to Scripture, a life must be taken (blood must be shed) for forgiveness to occur, "For the life of a creature is in the blood, and I have given it to you to make atonement for yourselves on the altar; it is the blood that makes atonement for one's life" (Leviticus 17:11 NIV). In the New Testament book of Hebrews, it states that all things are cleansed with blood: "And according to the Law, one may almost say, all things are cleansed with blood, and without shedding of blood there is no forgiveness" (Hebrews 9:22).

God forgave the sin of eating the forbidden fruit by taking a life of an animal and shedding the first blood to cover up their nakedness with skins to cover over their sin. The word for this is *atonement*, which means to cover. God covered Adam and Eve with animal skins; therefore, He covered their sin with blood, "The LORD God made garments of skin for Adam and his wife, and clothed them" (Genesis 3:21).

With the punishment came the promise.

Where Hope is Found

God's story, from the very beginning, foreshadowed His game plan in the form of a seed that sprouted hope for mankind. "And I will put enmity between you and the woman, and between your seed and her seed; He shall bruise you on the head, and you shall bruise him on the heel" (Genesis 3:15). In the struggle, hope was found.

> This is the first gospel sermon that was ever delivered upon the surface of the earth. It was memorable discourse indeed, with Jehovah himself for the preacher, and the whole human race and the prince of darkness for the audience. It must be worthy of our heartiest attention. ~Charles Spurgeon, *Christ the Conqueror of Satan* [4]

Each one of our stories contains a struggle. Your struggles may be different from your best friends' struggles, but we each have them. They are a part of our stories. In the struggle is where hope is found. In the greatest story, the fall is the conflict, or struggle, that sets the stage for the gospel.

Satan, disguised as the serpent, had bruised the heel of the seed of the woman (Jesus); however, in the end, the seed of the woman will crush the head of the serpent with a fatal blow. Many commentators refer to this seed as redeemed humanity in the body of Jesus Christ, "The carnal seed of the man and the woman are not meant, but the spiritual seed, even Christ Jesus and those who are in him" Charles Spurgeon, *Christ the Conqueror*.[5] In other words, the promise of a Redeemer is the spiritual seed.

This seed was promised to Adam and Eve, and according to the New Testament genealogies of Jesus, is passed down through their descendant Seth into the hearts of the Hebrew people and a select few Gentiles who had a heart for God. From the one seed a root system for one nation and one people group is established.

Satan bruises Christ by causing His physical death on earth, but just as a bruise is not final, neither was Christ's death on the cross. Christ did not stay dead. Christ rose from the dead and one day Christ will come again! The seed of the serpent, or spiritual descendants of Satan, will be crushed, ultimately defeated, and eventually they will all be thrown into the Lake of Fire.[6] "The God of peace will soon crush Satan under your feet" (Romans 16:20a).

The struggle for the seed's survival is a part of each one of our stories, intricately woven into the greatest story, to ultimately bring righteousness to all.

The Champion Within

We all have weaknesses that draw us away from righteousness. You can be sure, the adversary knows your weakness. Just as he knew how to reach Eve, he knows how to reach you. In his craftiness, he has studied your life. As a result, he knows how to specifically tempt you. Each one of our temptations is different, but you can know for certain that the battle for your soul began in the beginning of time. You are not alone. When you are feeling the tension of the struggle within, you can know that the struggle is real.

In the beginning, enmity was born between you and the adversary. However, when you understand the depth of God's love, believe in Him, repent (turn back to Him) and receive Jesus as your Savior, a Champion is born in you.[7] The Champion is the Holy Spirit, who comforts, guides, and fights every battle, seen and unseen, for you.

The moment you believe, God plants the spiritual seed within you and immediately you become a threat to the darkness. When the free gift of the Holy Spirit is born in you, you are declared righteous. God gives you mercy and extends grace. In your weakness, the Holy Spirit gives you strength. In your isolation, the Holy Spirit gives you love. In your anxiety, the Holy Spirit gives you peace, and His light shines from within you.

Just because the Champion has been born within you does not mean that the adversary is finished. In fact, he will continue to nip at your heel for the rest of your life. This is the result of the enmity established at the fall of humanity. Remember, he knows your weaknesses. You are not alone. We all have them. The adversary knows how to deceive us.

Deception is Satan's primary strategy. He will try to lead you away from God's truth and deceive you into believing his lies. To combat His attacks, we must take every thought captive to Christ.[7] Our weaknesses cause us to be curious. If we take those thoughts captive, we will shift our focus from self to Savior in order to satisfy our curiosity.

To become truly free, you must surrender.
~John Ortberg, *Soul Keeping* [8]

Freedom in Christ

At this point, you might think, *"So what? Eve was the one who ate the fruit! Why do I need to turn back to God because of her sin?"*

Through our spiritual lineage, Eve's sin directly affects you and me. Every newborn baby is born with a sin nature as a result of the original sin. Before we even make one mistake of our own, the sin nature is present, and from the moment of our earliest awareness, we continue to mess up daily.

On our own, we lack the wisdom to discern what is sin and what is not. In our minds, there is always a "gray area" to grapple with. *Am I giving my children enough attention, or am I giving them too much attention? Have I said something unkind, or raised my voice? Have I stood up for my faith or blended into the crowd? How about alcohol? Food? Money? Addictions? How much is too much?* We continue to mess up, but there is hope.

God whispers to your soul in His perfect timing, *"I exchanged my Son for you ... He was beaten, shamed, and bled as the final sacrifice. His blood was poured out for you. Your sins are washed away, so that we can be together as one again."* You are covered with the blood of His Son and when God looks at you, that's what He sees.

Your life has changed. You are a new creation. No longer is life about what you do or don't do; it's about what the power of the Holy Spirit does through you. Through our belief in Jesus Christ, the spiritual seed is birthed, a relationship with God is established, and the gift of eternal life is received.

That perfect timing is described in this verse written by the Apostle Paul. In it, Paul describes God's powerful process of finding freedom, to bear the fruit that leads to eternal life: "But now you are free from the power of sin and have become slaves of God. Now you do those things that lead to holiness and result in eternal life" (Romans 6:22 NLT).

When God calls us back to Himself, He frees us of our past — the sin past we were born with from Adam and Eve, and the sin past we created on our own. Doesn't freedom sound wonderful? No longer are we slaves to sin, but rather servants of the most Holy God who gives us the precious gift of eternal life, through the blood of His very own Son.

Has the seed taken up residence in your heart? Another man or woman cannot grow it for you. God alone passes down the life of the seed and grows it in the hearts of those whom He loves. The moment you believe, He places you directly into His family tree and connects you to His deep roots.

*No longer is life about
what you do or don't do; it's about
what the power of the Holy Spirit
does through you.*

By yourself, you cannot do anything to make yourself perfectly clean and sinless. Although many of us love the idea of being perfect, sometimes we need to let it go. No matter how hard we try, neither you nor I will ever be able to do enough to earn a place in His clean, sinless, perfect presence. Only Jesus was perfect and sinless from the beginning. His perfect blood covers up our imperfections and makes us new, holy, and righteous. Each one of our scars is a beautiful reminder of our own curiosity that propelled us into the struggle, which ultimately led us right to the heart of the Father.

Obedience and Blessing

The adversary shows up when you least expect him to. In Christ, the power of God helps you overcome the battle set before you. When you believe in Christ, God gives you the free gift of the Holy Spirit. You are gifted with the power of God, and it is the Spirit of the living God who gently guides you through each struggle.

An intense struggle between my flesh and the Spirit came upon me when Jon's father passed away. The family decided to spread his father's ashes in the Indian Ocean where Jon grew up, and where he and his father spent many hours fishing. Jon's mom wanted to return to Africa for closure. Jon wanted to introduce me to the continent he loves. However, our children, ages three and one, were too young to endure the trip with us. At that time, I could not imagine leaving my children behind for two weeks while we traveled to the other side of the world. My husband needed me by his side, yet my heartstrings were tied tightly to my young children. I had just finished nursing my daughter, and during that tender season, I was able be at home with her during the day. My children were my life, passion, and purpose. But this dilemma brought me face-to-face with the truth that first I had a commitment to God and the covenant of marriage with my husband.

I prayed and prayed about the situation. I did not want to go, but I knew I needed to be present for my husband. Prayer embraced my soul, convicted me that it was God's will for me to go, and the Holy Spirit filled me with the strength to obey. I packed my bags and traveled to the other side of the world without my babies. Before I left, I sang the lyrics to the song, "He's got the whole world in His hands" to my daughter as she lay sweetly and peacefully on my chest. I was at peace.

The struggle had been real, present, and alive in my life, but God's presence in my life was larger than my fear. The reward I received was the priceless gift of oneness, a bond like glue, within my covenant marriage, a bond that is stronger than the deceiver who strives to break our marriages all into pieces.

Jon and I were gone for ten days. In that time, I saw and experienced the heart of my husband which flourished in his beloved Tanzania. We visited his school and the pool where he still held the fastest swimming record, the house behind stone walls and guards where he grew up, and the markets he had shopped in. We probably even saw some of the same animals, just a few years older, that he had seen on safari as a teenager! We released his father's ashes in the Indian Ocean, and I was able to be completely present in that once-in-a-lifetime experience — beside my husband, his mom, and his sister. Our time together was precious and priceless, and I'm so grateful I obeyed God, the Lover of my soul.

In the midst of our struggles, you and I can trust that the Creator always has our best interest in mind. In my early marriage-versus-parenting struggle, God indelibly marked this principle upon my heart: With loyalty and obedience to the Lover of my soul come great blessings. This was a turning point, a climacteric, defining moment for me.

I recently had to remind myself of this lesson when my husband asked me to go on a two-week marketing and recruiting trip to China. Our purpose in China would be to advertise our school and interview students to come study with us. Once again, Jon was suggesting that I leave my children behind and travel to the other side of the world with him and a group of school administrators. Okay, I know most women would jump at the chance to travel with their husband, even if it was on business, however, the timing was really difficult for me.

It didn't feel like a good time to be gone for two entire weeks in the middle of the semester. Oblivious to my previous lesson learned, my natural reaction again did not put my marriage first. Once again, the struggle between flesh and Spirit overwhelmed my soul. I prayed fervently in the following days. The Holy Spirit quietly broke through my anxiety. His peaceful voice reminded me, "With loyalty and obedience to the Lover of my soul come great blessings." The Spirit reminded me what God did for us when we were in Africa together. I knew then that God wanted me to honor my marriage and my husband by going to China, even though it was more than inconvenient.

With loyalty and obedience
to the Lover of my soul come great blessings.

To be fair, part of my hesitation for not going to China was because the health of my beloved grandfather, whom my children called Popee Dave, was declining quickly. I knew he probably would pass away while I was gone, but I also knew that I had to be there for my husband. After talking the decision over with my precious grandmother, I made time to visit my grandfather one last time. His weary body was fading fast.

I sat beside my grandfather in the nursing home and held his hand as he told me his stories for the last time. He spoke of how much he loved my grandmother, his children, his grandchildren, and his great-grandchildren. Out of reverence for the Lord, he put on his kippa, and we recited Psalm 23 together. He passed me a book of

Jewish prayers. We talked about the devotionals I had been writing daily for my family and for him for the past two years. During that season of writing, my grandfather was my biggest fan and strongest encourager. He read each and every devotional. He called me often to tell me he read the devotional and told me each one was beautiful. He always said that each devotional spoke to his heart. He said to me, "You and I, we have something very special. We believe."

Our last bedside conversation led to a beautiful discussion. We talked about how God's beloved Son became the last sacrifice for each one of us — once and for all. We talked about repentance. We talked about how our belief in Jesus gives us new life — a life that is eternal. My Jewish grandfather and I prayed together in the precious name of Jesus. Joy emerged in my heart at his bedside. I know I will see my beloved grandfather again in eternity.

Shortly after that visit I left for China with a joy-filled heart, yet with tears filling my eyes, I once again reminded myself that God holds the whole-wide world in His hands — as I had done when I sang the same words to my daughter years ago. Just as I had feared, while Jon and I were on the other side of the world, my grandfather went home to be with the Lord.

The morning of my Grandfather's funeral stateside, it was twelve hours later in China. While quietly grieving, one of the administrators I was with pointed out the beautiful lights overhead. I glanced up and saw one cross with eight lights, which looked just like a Jewish menorah, behind it. My heavenly Father was smiling on me and the peace that transcends all understanding filled my weary soul.

The Olive Tree: Rooted, *Part 2*

Because of Adam and Eve's sin, and the legacy of their nature, our curiosity continues to lead us away from the Source of all goodness and truth. God gives us the ability to choose and we are filled with curiosity, which He hopes will lead us back to Himself. Throughout the stories in the Old Testament, the Hebrew nation continued to choose to worship, rebel, repent, and repeat, and yet God loved them.

Regardless, God protected the Hebrew nation and even "guarded him as the pupil of his eye" (Deut. 32:10). In return, the nation of Israel was to honor and serve the Father and be a light to the Gentiles

(Isaiah 42:6; 60:3). The nation was God's firstborn son. "When Israel was a youth I loved him, and out of Egypt I called My son" (Hosea 11:1).[9] Through Israel, the imperishable seed was established and carried within the roots of each generation.

Then there was a period of silence. God became silent for 400 years — the tree was cut back to a stump. "For there is hope for a tree, when it is cut down, that it will sprout again, and its shoots will not fail" (Job 14:7).

However, embedded within the stump was the seed of hope. "Yet there will be a tenth portion in it, and it will again be subject to burning, like a terebinth or an oak whose stump remains when it is felled. The holy seed is its stump" (Isaiah 6:13).

Once again, even in the silence, God was present.

TREASURE, PRAYER, AND REFLECTION

Scripture Treasure

"And we know that God causes all things to work together for good to those who love God, to those who are called according to His purpose" (Romans 8:28).

Praying God's Promises

Heavenly Father,

I praise You for who You are. I praise You because Your seed, Jesus, from the beginning of time, established Your deep roots. I praise You for sending Your Son to defeat the adversary in my life. When I believe, the Spirit is born in me, and I have a Champion fighting for me. The struggles in my life are real, but I know You overcame the cross, and You will be the victor in the end. I am grateful to You for fighting the battles I see and for fighting the battles that I cannot see. Thank You for showing me how my struggles are a valuable part of my story, as they take me deeper into a relationship with You. Thank You for teaching me that anyone, at any age, may come into a relationship with You.

In Your precious name, Jesus, I pray,
Amen

Spiritual Discipline: *Read God's Word*

It is important to read some of God's Word every day. "For the word of God is living and active and sharper than any two-edged sword, and piercing as far as the division of soul and spirit, of both joints and marrow, and able to judge the thoughts and intentions of the heart" (Hebrews 4:12). Remember, *Beautiful Legacy* is merely an arrow pointing you to the Bible. You may begin with a book such as this one or a devotional, but those books are only meant to point you to the truth of God's living and active Word, otherwise known as the Bible. The Bible is where the ancient foundational words of our faith are found.

Deep Roots Reflection
Old Testament Word: *zera* (Hebrew)
seed, sowing, offspring, descendants, of moral quality [10]

The seed, passed from the beginning of time, through descendants of Adam and Eve, carries the spiritual life, which is born in our believing hearts today. A seed can only produce a tree of its own kind.

Look up the following verses and write them in the spaces provided. Then take time to answer the questions.

Galatians 6:7-8 ~

God knows where your desire is placed. Are the desires for things of this world greater than Him in your life right now?

Romans 4:18 ~

Abraham rested in the hope of God to unfold the rest of his own story, which seemed impossible. Is there a part of your life in which you need to rest in the hope of God? _______________________________

How does it feel to know you have a Champion within you who fought for you, defeated death, and continues to fight for you today?

____

____

____

____

____

God is sinless. He does not tolerate sin in His presence. How does this make you feel? Do you need to repent or get rid of something before you enter into God's presence, or open up His Word today? "Therefore, since we have so great a cloud of witnesses surrounding us, let us also lay aside every encumbrance and the sin which so easily entangles us, and let us run with endurance the race that is set before us" (Hebrews 12:1).

____

____

____

____

____

According to scripture, life is found in the blood. In order for forgiveness to occur, a life must be sacrificed. God gave Adam and Eve a covering made of animal skins (Genesis 3:21). The word atonement means, "to cover." What does this mean in relationship to the blood of Christ?

____

____

____

____

____

How does it feel to know His blood has covered all of your sins?

____

____

____

____

____

God forgives, but that does not mean there will not be consequences. Consequences keep us from traveling down the same undesirable path a second time. God continues to put boundaries in place for our own safety and protection. Scars remind us of when we crossed those boundaries, but they do heal, and we become whole again. Hallelujah!

Every decision we make either reflects or deflects His glory. May we steadfastly choose to glorify and please Him, our dear Heavenly Father. When we make mistakes, God is faithful to give us uncomfortable discipline. God disciplines those He loves, "So that He may establish your hearts without blame in holiness before our God and Father at the coming of our Lord Jesus with all His saints" (1 Thess. 3:13).

Beautiful Legacy Reminder

God cultivates our hearts through struggles, which are a part of our story. A seed may be born in a cultivated heart. Scars are reminders of our own curiosity, which led us into the struggle, but they give us wisdom to seek God. God's mercy and provision of a Savior instills hope and growth — and a way back to the heart of the Father.

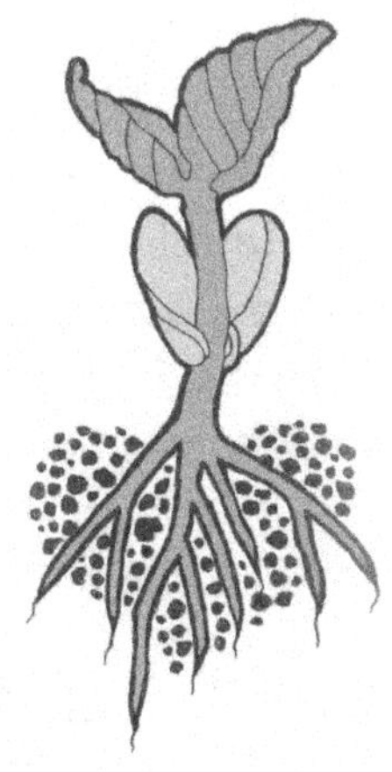

CHAPTER FOUR

Brilliant

O Holy Spirit, descend plentifully into my heart.
Enlighten the dark corners of this neglected dwelling
and scatter there Thy cheerful beams.
~ St. Augustine [1]

Our God is more concerned about your connection to Him than your comfort in this world. Today's circumstances, or what you currently see, are only temporary. Don't get too comfortable, because God will pick you up and move you right out of that little comfort zone you are sitting in right now.

At the beginning of our marriage, God moved us from two comfortable, well-paying jobs in Virginia to two much smaller jobs in Florida within a tiny private school. He moved us from our new, single-family home in the suburbs of Washington, D.C. to a tiny two-bedroom apartment in the middle of an orange grove. We did not know what He was doing at the time, but we knew there was something more than what we could see and understand with our own eyes and hearts. While we could see only a snapshot of our story, we had to completely trust that it fit perfectly within God's big picture of the greatest story.

Trusting God does not always come easily. However, when we take a look at the big picture that we fit into, it helps us trust Him. He was present in the beginning of time, He is present today, and He will be present with you tomorrow until the end of time (Hebrews 13:8).

When our hearts let go of anxiety in order for His peace to take residence, He works through us in amazing ways. God chooses people who have a heart for Him to accomplish the work He needs to do in order for Him to receive the glory.

> *When our hearts let go of anxiety*
> *in order for His peace to take residence,*
> *He works through us in amazing ways.*

There are many ways God uses ordinary people as He places them uncomfortably outside of their comfort zones and into His comfort zone. You may be asked to travel to a distant place, befriend a stranger to whom you would never normally speak, try a new routine, go on a diet, or He may prompt you to do something even more unusual which is completely out of your comfort zone, yet completely in His.

I was on bed rest expecting our first child when I heard God whisper to me, "I'm going to grow you in a different way." Jon and I had made that first move from Virginia to Florida completely trusting God's guidance and provision. We left behind our home and the comfort of our family and friends to follow Him. Because of this dramatic leap of faith and since God was our constant when everything else in the world had changed, God grew our young hearts together spiritually. If we had not made that initial move out of our comfort zone, our relationship with Him would not be where it is today, and we would not be where we are today.

We slowly learned that comfort is not found in a place, but rather in a Person. He guides us and teaches us according to God's perfect plan. "But the Comforter, which is the Holy Ghost, whom the Father will send in my name, he shall teach you all things, and bring all things to your remembrance, whatsoever I have said unto you" (John 14:26 KJV).

Knowing that I am not alone on my journey, as you are not alone in yours, brings me comfort in uncomfortable places. Stories of men and women who have gone before us set examples for you and me to follow. And always, when we look at our stories in hindsight, we, too, can always see the fingerprints of God. Our stories will someday be an example to those who follow in our footsteps, most likely, our children and children's children.

We learned that comfort is not found in a place,
but rather in a Person.

Each hero of the faith has a story that gives us a greater glimpse of God's perfect guidance and His perfect provision out of His perfect plan. Stories of broken people restored by a perfect God fill the Bible so we can understand that we are not alone in our faith walk. Just as the prophet Isaiah reminded the Hebrew people, he reminds us today that God's thoughts about us are not our thoughts, they are higher.

> For My thoughts are not your thoughts, nor are your ways My ways,' declares the LORD. 'For as the heavens are higher than the earth, so are My ways higher than your ways and My thoughts than your thoughts (Isaiah 55:8-9).

Stories of broken people restored by a perfect God
fill the Bible so we can understand that
we are not alone in our faith walk.

Since we know God keeps His promises, we can trust that He will use our individual, unique journeys to make us more like Him. He doesn't expect or demand perfection of us. We can't be perfect; that's why He sent His Son to the cross. Our sanctification, becoming like Christ, is a lifelong process until we get to heaven and are completely transformed. But here on earth, His work in us is leading us toward

His perfection. Philippians 1:6 says, "For I am confident of this very thing, that He who began a good work in you will perfect it until the day of Christ Jesus."

Trust

Remember, God lived in the oneness of community from the very beginning. Just as Jesus was with God in the beginning, the Spirit of God was with Him in the beginning, too. "Now the earth was formless and empty, darkness was over the surface of the deep, and the Spirit of God was hovering over the waters" (Genesis 1:2 NIV).

They were three in one. All three persons of the Trinity can see the big picture — from the beginning of time to the very end. When we understand this, we can trust Him when we cannot see.

*God lived in community
from the very beginning.*

God placed the imperishable seed right into the life of Abram. Abram could not see where God was sending him, but Abram chose to follow God. Abram took his family out of the metropolis of Ur, away from his relatives and his father's home, to an unknown land. God would make Abram's land great, and through Abram all of the earth would be blessed (Genesis 12:1-3). Abram received this promise directly from God and trusted Him.

He Believed

Genesis 15:18 says that God "cut a covenant" (or made an agreement) with Abram and Sara. According to the original Hebrew wording, a covenant, or *beriyth*, is a divine ordinance between God and man, complete with pledges and signs. Just as God first placed the breath of life into Adam, "Then the LORD God formed man of dust from the ground, and breathed into his nostrils the breath of life; and man became a living being" (Genesis 2:7). Some commentators believe God symbolically gave Abram new life when He took the H, representing His breath, directly from His own name, YHWH, and placed it into their names. Abram and Sara became Abraham and Sarah, and new life began.

Abraham's name went from meaning "exalted father" to "the father of a multitude of nations." Through his belief, Abraham established his faith and allegiance to God. "Then he believed in the LORD; and He reckoned it to him as righteousness" (Genesis 15:6).

When we commit ourselves to God,
He breathes His life of the Holy Spirit into us.

Names are significant. The sign of Abraham's faith was his name change. A name change signifies a changed life and destiny. This concept is the same for us today. When we commit ourselves to God, He breathes His life of the Holy Spirit into us. Our name may not change, but our identity and destiny change. God breathes life into us by the power of the Holy Spirit. This new life connects us to Him as one. He tells us, "I am my beloved's and my beloved is mine" (Song of Solomon 6:3a).

This new life connects both Jews and Gentiles as one with our ancestor, Abraham, who received the blessing many years ago. The Spirit gave new life to Abraham, just as the Spirit gives us new life when we believe.

Dear friend, don't miss this: When God cut covenant with Abraham, He declared Abraham as righteous, gave him the breath of life, and a nation was born. God breathes life into us just as He breathed life into Abraham and into the dry bones in Ezekiel's valley. God made those still, dry bones come to life by breathing the Spirit of the Living God into them (Ezekiel 37:1-14).

The Birth of a Nation

Abram descended from Adam, but grew up with a father who was distant from the one true God. Yet God knew He could use Abram. God blessed him and promised him through his seed that his descendants would outnumber the stars in the sky, " '... a son who is your own flesh and blood will be your heir.' He took him outside and said, 'Look up at the sky and count the stars—if indeed you can count them.' Then he said to him, 'So shall your offspring be.' " (Genesis 15:4b-5).

Through the people of Abraham, God promised that He would bless all of the nations on the earth. In the book of Romans, Paul explains, "and not all are children of Abraham because they are his offspring, but 'Through Isaac shall your offspring be named.' This means that it is not the children of the flesh who are the children of God, but the children of the promise are counted as offspring" (Romans 9:7-8 ESV).

Abraham's seed established the nation for the sake of all nations. Abraham's son Isaac married Rebekah, and in a world full of darkness, Jacob, who would later be called Israel, was born. God chose Israel to shine the light for all other nations to see. Passed as a legacy from Jewish parents to their children, the spiritual seed established deep roots within the faith-family tree and kept the bloodline going. Under God's protection and guidance, the small nation grew and thrived. When the nation of Israel was hard-pressed, God's light beamed the brightest.

The Covenant of the Law

God blessed Israel as the twelve tribes were birthed through him. Their story places God's chosen nation into an uncomfortable place in order for His purpose to be fulfilled. God used Joseph, son of Rachel, and Israel's beloved son, to preserve the nation through a famine. In God's adventurous story for Joseph, he traveled from the pit to the prison and then ultimately rose to Pharaoh's palace. God used Joseph's hard-pressed life to preserve His seed. The Hebrew people thrived in the foreign land until a new Pharaoh arrived, and they fell into bondage as God had told Abraham they would (Genesis 15:13). This 400-year bondage lasted until the Lord sent a baby down the Nile right into the arms of Pharaoh's family.

That baby, Moses, was sent to pull the nation of Israel out of Egypt. In God's perfect timing, God was present from Moses' birth through his path to leadership. God never rests, and just like in Moses' story, the snapshot of your story is a part of the greatest story. God's fingerprints are on all our lives — weaving together our yesterday, today, and our tomorrow.

God proved His sovereignty to the children of Israel and the people of Egypt through ten plagues that decimated the Egyptians, but did not bother the Hebrews. From blood to frogs to locusts to hail, and finally to darkness, Moses asked Pharaoh to release the Hebrew people so they could worship their God in the wilderness (Exodus 5:1), but the hard-hearted Pharaoh would not let them go. The first nine plagues God sent did not convince Pharaoh, so God sent a plague like no other. For this final plague to pass over the Hebrews, God told each family they would have to slay a young, innocent lamb. God told Moses to tell the Hebrews to use the blood of the lamb to paint the doorposts of their homes. Any firstborn child behind a door that was not covered by the blood became a victim to the angel of death.

When God does something big, you need 
to mark it down, in order to remember.

This final plague pierced Pharaoh's heart; for when it passed, a dead child lay in every Egyptian home, including the palace. Pharaoh finally told the Hebrews to go and worship their God. They left Egypt with all of their flocks and herds, and they plundered the Egyptians on their way, never to return. Through Moses, God delivered the twelve tribes of Israel out of bondage. They were finally free. The hand of God could only have done this. "Moses said to the people, 'Remember this day in which you went out from Egypt, from the house of slavery; for by a powerful hand the LORD brought you out from this place'" (Exodus 13:3a).

Today, the holiday of Passover, otherwise known in the Hebrew culture as the Festival of Redemption, reminds the Hebrew people of when the angel of death passed over their homes and God delivered the nation out of Egyptian bondage.

The Seder, or special meal eaten to celebrate Passover, in the home of my grandparents many years ago, introduced me to the prophet Elijah, and the study of it sparked my curiosity about where the roots of our faith-family tree began.

Jewish families share the Seder meal every year to remember. The Seder meal is what led me to begin asking questions. Where did it all begin? We remember, so that we may know. We know, so that we may remember. When God does something big, you need to mark it down, in order to remember.

Lest we forget … Israel's children traveled through the wilderness for forty years while God prepared their hearts for the promised land. In the wilderness, God reminded Moses of His sovereignty and gave the ten commands to him in order to help establish order within the young nation (Exodus 20:2-17).

God creates and establishes His people and His directions with great love in an organized fashion, because our Heavenly Father can see the big picture, "Now then, if you will indeed obey My voice and keep My covenant, then you shall be My own possession among all the peoples, for all the earth is Mine" (Exodus 19:5-6).

God wrote the ten commands with Moses and the people committed to follow Him and all of His ways. "Then Moses came and recounted to the people all the words of the LORD and all the ordinances; and all the people answered with one voice and said, 'All the words which the LORD has spoken we will do!' " (Exodus 24:3).

The commands taught holiness and established boundaries for the new nation's own safety and protection. However, our human hearts have a hard time keeping up with strict rules. Don't put anything before the Lord, don't take the Lord's name in vain, do not steal, don't want any more than the Lord has already provided, no, no, no. Each one of us has broken at least one, two, or five, or more. Jesus even says that if you sin in your heart, you are guilty (Matthew 5:21-30). Although this does not give us an excuse to not try to meet them, these commands of the old covenant establish the fact that humans are not perfect, which shines the light on why God sent a perfect Savior.

 *Deep roots were what grounded their faith.*

The covenant of the law was exactly what the new nation needed at the time, "Why the Law then? It was added because of transgressions, having been ordained through angels by the agency of the mediator, until the seed would come to whom the promise had been made" (Galatians 3:19). Through the Hebrew nation, the seed continued to travel from generation to generation. Deep roots were what grounded their faith.

The Light

God knows our struggles better than we know them ourselves. He walks through the darkness with us. Often, we don't understand what is happening within or around us, because we cannot see behind the scenes. As a child faced with fear leans into a father with trust, we press into our Heavenly Father for strength and hope. According to His Word, we know that, "God is light, and in Him there is no darkness at all" (1 John 1:5).

Our Father sovereignly selects those whom He knows will help Him carry out His purposes. The young Hebrew maiden, Hadassah, more commonly known as Esther, was a young girl when God called her (Esther 2). Mordecai raised Esther, the daughter of his uncle, to know the God of Abraham, Isaac, and Jacob. She was a virgin whose heart was as pure as her body.

After the removal of the original queen, God strategically placed Esther into the arms of the Persian king, King Xerxes: "The king loved Esther more than all the women, and she found favor and kindness with him more than all the virgins, so that he set the royal crown on her head and made her queen instead of Vashti" (Esther 2:17). The king loved his new queen Esther, but he did not know her ancestry (Esther 2:10, 2:20). It turns out that this influential king, King Xerxes, became a pivotal figure in the history of the Hebrew nation's preservation.

Every good story has a struggle caused by an antagonist. In Esther's story, the antagonist is the adversary who came in the form of an arrogant man named Haman. The king promoted Haman, "but Mordecai neither bowed down nor paid homage," to the proud leader, Haman (Esther 3:2). Mordecai's nonconformity was a threat to Haman's leadership. So Haman wanted to destroy Mordecai. And Haman took his hatred even further. He wanted to completely eradicate the people Mordecai represented. Haman was going after the entire Jewish nation (Esther 3:6).

Little did Haman know that Mordecai had a strategic connection in the palace — Queen Esther herself. Haman went to the king to present the case for what he felt was a treasonous element in the kingdom. He told the king about a certain people group who had different laws "from those of all other people and they do not observe the king's laws, so it is not in the king's interest to let them remain" (Esther 3:8). As a result, "Letters were sent by couriers to all the king's provinces to destroy, to kill and to annihilate all the Jews, both young and old, women and children, in one day" (Esther 3:13).

When Mordecai found out about the edict sent to annihilate the Jews, he went to Esther to inform her so that she could go to the king to "plead ... for her people" (Esther 4:8). Esther responded by saying she could not approach the king without being summoned or she could be put to death (Esther 4:11). Mordecai pleads with Esther to use her position to help her people, even though it meant putting herself in mortal danger. Mordecai then asks a desperate question: "And who knows whether you have not attained royalty for such a time as this?" (Esther 4:14).

Realizing the severity of the situation, Esther agrees to help. She tells Mordecai to instruct the Jews to fast and pray. She says that she and her attendants will fast with them, and then she bravely declares, "if I perish, I perish" (Esther 4:16). She was willing to lose her life rather than refuse to be used by God.

Esther's position as a Jew in the Persian castle proves to be the key to preservation of the nation. In the middle of a dark plight, the story of young Queen Esther unfolded.

The king's affections for his virtuous wife, Esther, defeated the adversary in his tracks. Haman was revealed to Xerxes as the proud, crooked servant he was. To right the situation, King Xerxes could not go back on the edict that he had already sent to annihilate the Hebrew nation, since it had been sealed with his signet ring. But he did send a second decree. The second decree allowed for the nation of Israel to prepare and fight back. In the ensuing day of fighting, the Israelites were victorious, and to this day, they continue to celebrate the victory they found through Esther in a holiday called Purim.

The story of Esther and the holiday of Purim resonate deep within my heart. I remember sitting in temple while the story of Esther was read. It was a long and loud service. This reading at synagogue is time consuming since every time Haman's name is mentioned, the congregation makes noise by shouting and yelling against the evil he represents. We would also celebrate Purim by eating triangle cookies known as Haman's hats. It was a time of victorious joy!

Each one of us has or has had a Haman in our lives. The adversary works through people who are walking according to the flesh. We all have someone who has come against us and spoken harshly to us or instilled seeds of doubt.

Remember, you have the seed of a Savior who created you to be a champion. The Champion, the Holy Spirit, shines brighter in you than any Haman in your life. Where there is death, there is a need for life. "Then Jesus again spoke to them, saying, 'I am the Light of the world; he who follows Me will not walk in the darkness, but will have the Light of life'" (John 8:12). Where there is darkness, there is a need for light. The Light of the world provides life to the world. "For this reason it says, 'Awake, sleeper, and arise from the dead, and Christ will shine on you'" (Ephesians 5:14).

Remember, you have the seed of a Savior who created you to be a champion. The Champion, the Holy Spirit, shines brighter in you than any Haman in your life. Where there is death, there is a need for life.

The Olive Tree: *The Shoot*

The imperishable seed was preserved and traveled through the Hebrew people from Adam to Abraham to Moses to Esther into Jesse and the heart of his son, King David, until a new tree shoot grew right through the silence and into the heart of the noble lineage. "Then a shoot will spring from the stem of Jesse, and a branch from his roots will bear fruit" (Isaiah 11:1).

From the beginning of time, the One who came through the shoot traveled through the roots of God's faith-family tree. He grew up in an ordinary, everyday, Jewish home, "For He grew up before Him like a tender shoot, and like a root out of parched ground; He has no stately form or majesty that we should look upon Him, nor appearance that we should be attracted to Him" (Isaiah 53:2). The world didn't recognize Him. "He was in the world, and the world was made through Him, and the world did not know Him" (John 1:10).

Then when Jesus was alive, he introduced the new covenant that was to come for all people. "And when He had taken some bread and given thanks, He broke it and gave it to them, saying, 'This is My body which is given for you; do this in remembrance of Me.' And in the same way He took the cup after they had eaten, saying, 'This cup which is poured out for you is the new covenant in My blood' (Luke 22:19-20)."

We remember the greatest sacrifice who was given once and for all, and we give thanks, "Is not the cup of blessing that we bless a sharing in the blood of Christ? Is not the bread which we break a sharing in the body of Christ?" (1 Corinthians 10:16).

Jesus, the seed of hope that traveled through the generations of the Hebrew people, was revealed to the world in God's perfect timing. His death and resurrection split time and ushered in the new covenant of grace to both Jews and Gentiles who recognized themselves in Him.

Jesus, the seed of hope that traveled through the generations of the Hebrew people, was revealed to the world in God's perfect timing.

TREASURE, PRAYER, AND REFLECTION

Scripture Treasure

"For this reason it says, 'Awake, sleeper, and arise from the dead, and Christ will shine on you'" (Ephesians 5:14).

Praying God's Promises

Heavenly Father,

I praise You for sending the Light to a dark world. Thank You for giving us a way to see You. Thank You for shining the Light of eternal hope into my heart. Thank You for showing me that You are with me always. I am never alone. Help me turn back to You. As You continue to shine Your Light, enlighten me so the darkness and lies of this world will be dispelled by the radiance of Your truth.

In Your precious name, Jesus, I pray,
Amen

Spiritual Discipline: *Fasting*

Esther fasted with the Jewish nation before she approached the King. She needed clear discernment for the direction she was to take. Fasting puts our focus on God for strength and sustenance. Jesus told his disciples to fast:

Whenever you fast, do not put on a gloomy face as the hypocrites do, for they neglect their appearance so that they will be noticed by men when they are fasting. Truly I say to you, they have their reward in full. But you, when you fast, anoint your head and wash your face so that your fasting will not be noticed by men, but by your Father who is in secret; and your Father who sees what is done in secret will reward you (Matthew 6:16-18).

The many different ways of fasting include the following: not eating one meal, not eating from sunup to sundown, or eliminating one food from your diet. Some people will even fast without water. Some people will allow for water to be included in their fast. Fasting takes us out of our comfort zone. Fasting humbles the soul and allows for one to focus on God.

Deep Roots Reflection
Old Testament Word: *beriyth* (Hebrew)
covenant, allegiance, pledge, divine ordinance[2]
The Bible is divided into two covenants: The Old Covenant is called the covenant of the law, while The New Covenant is called the covenant of grace.

Look up the following verses and write them in the spaces provided. Then take time to answer the following questions.

Galatians 4:22-26 ~

____

____

____

____

____

When you believe, you enter into the covenant of grace and become a child of the promise, which means that you are born, not in a natural way, but by the power of God. How does it make you feel to know you are now a child of the promise God once made to Abraham when He told him that his descendants would be as numerous as the stars in the sky (Genesis 15:5)?

____

____

____

____

____

Matthew 26:26-28 ~

____

____

____

How do these verses show the price Jesus paid for the new covenant?

____

____

____

____

What covenants (or agreements) do you have in your life?

____

____

____

____

____

____

____

God is the ultimate covenant maker. When you place your trust in God, He creates a covenant relationship with you. God never breaks His Word. Abraham knew this promise. Moses knew this promise. Esther knew this promise. Jesus fulfills this promise. God was with them. Just as you and I become scared at times, they were scared, too. They had to live with bravery and courage. That courage came from their rock-solid belief in their covenant-keeping God. The blood of Jesus covered the law, and the new covenant of grace is made complete in the hearts of those who believe.

Regardless of where you are, His covenant stands. It never changes. Have you committed your life to Him in order to create a covenant with Him?

____

____

Sometimes God moves you from your comfort zone to an uncomfortable place in His comfort zone. In hindsight, are you able to see where He made the rough places smooth? "I will go before you and make the rough places smooth" (Isaiah 45:2).

____

____

"For I know the plans I have for you, declares the LORD" (Jeremiah 29:11). How has this verse above played out in your life?

____

____

____

____

"For such a time as this …" (Esther 4:14). What has God prepared you for, right now?

____

____

____

____

Has God used you to do something that only He could have done? How has God used you to do extraordinary things? If He hasn't, take time to pray for Him to reveal to you what He wants to do through you.

____

____

____

____

"If I perish, I perish" (Esther 4:16). If you were placed in a situation as difficult as Esther's, would you have the same strength and courage? What is going on in the world today that would lead you to believe you may have the opportunity to stand for your faith as Esther did?

____

____

____

____

"Then Jesus again spoke to them, saying, 'I am the Light of the world; he who follows Me will not walk in the darkness, but will have the Light of life'" (John 8:12).

God is Light.

Jesus is Light.

May His Light shine brilliantly through you.

Beautiful Legacy Reminder

God's plan for your life may not be comfortable, but you can trust He will bring you comfort along the way. Courage comes from standing on the Rock of our covenant-keeping God. God asks that we trust Him even when we cannot see and let His love shine brilliantly.

Jesus
QUEEN ESTHER
EZEKIEL
DAVID
MOSES
12 TRIBES OF ISRAEL
JACOB
ISHMAEL, ISAAC
ABRAHAM & SARAH
NOAH
ADAM & EVE
Father, SON & Holy Spirit
In the beginning was the Word, and the Word was
with God, and the Word was God (John 1:1).

Then a shoot will spring from the stem of Jesse, and a branch from his roots will bear fruit (Isaiah 11:1).

He was in the world, and the world was made through Him, and the world did not know Him (John 1:10).

... for you have been born again not of seed which is perishable but imperishable, that is, through the living and enduring word of God (1 Peter 1:23).

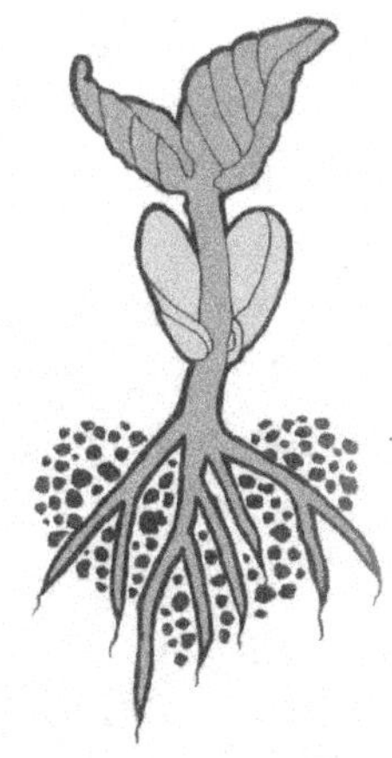

CHAPTER FIVE

Intimate

In intimacy with God,
he is able to hear the softest whispers of the Holy Spirit.
He learns to understand
the slightest sign of his Father's will and to follow it.
His strength continually increases,
for God is his strength and God is ever with him.
~ Andrew Murray[1]

On school nights, in order to prepare for my precious early morning quiet time with the Lover of my soul, I have learned to purposefully set the coffee pot for 5:30am. Then, when the morning skies are still dark, the smell of the strong brew makes its way upstairs and lures me out of bed and into the kitchen to pour my cup. Cradling the warm mug in my hands, I slip into my quiet office, my sacred space. In those dimly lit, quiet morning moments in my cozy desk chair, I savor the washing of the Word. As I read my Bible, the words come alive, the Holy Spirit strengthens my spirit and fills me deep within. Those precious minutes slip by quickly, and then it's time to wake the children.

And we're off!

We gather in our room for a family devotional, and then we scurry to get ready for school: make breakfast, finish lunches, gather backpacks, find volleyball kneepads, search for soccer cleats, locate football pads, and grab instruments. And hopefully, I have 30 seconds to spare to throw in a load of laundry!

I run out of my house, glance quickly at my flowers and realize the flowerbeds need to be weeded, and the grass is like a jungle. As I back my car out of the driveway, in my rearview mirror, I can see that even my roots need a touch-up! I can't remember if I made my bed, and I know it's time to clean the bathrooms again. My mind continues to spiral, and I panic, "Did I take the chicken out of the freezer for dinner tonight?"

In this ever-changing, crazy world,
I want to rely on a never-changing God.

From our children's tummies to the upkeep of our homes, how many things do you maintain in one day? Take 60 seconds and make a quick list in your head. It's amazing, isn't it? The innumerable to-do's of our modern life. The list always growing, hardly ever getting shorter. How easy it is to go from complete tranquility to panic at a moment's notice!

In this ever-changing, crazy world, I want to rely on a never-changing God.

20/20 Heart Vision

As the history of the Jewish nation progressed, God's generational roots multiplied and grew deep. They reached into the life of the prophet-judge Samuel; however, the Israelites wanted a king. Even though God told His people He was their King, their hearts desired a human king. They saw what the other nations around them had. They were not content with following their unseen God by faith. Instead, they wanted an earthly king to lead their nation.

Samuel appointed a handsome man, an outwardly impressive individual named Saul. But Saul did not follow God with all of his heart, so God did not let him complete his reign. Saul was not the one God wanted to continue to send the spiritual seed through in order to fulfill His promises. With a horn full of precious anointing oil, God sent Samuel to find the new ruddy-faced young king.

> Now the LORD said to Samuel, "How long will you grieve over Saul, since I have rejected him from being king over Israel? Fill your horn with oil and go; I will send you to Jesse the Bethlehemite, for I have selected a king for Myself among his sons" (1 Samuel 16:1).

By outward appearances, Jesse's first son looked like he could be the next chosen king. His stature was tall, dignified, and strong.

> But the Lord said to Samuel, "Do not look at his appearance or at the height of his stature, because I have rejected him; for God sees not as man sees, for man looks at the outward appearance, but the LORD looks at the heart" (1 Samuel 16:7).

Samuel listened to the Lord. He visited with Abinadab, then Shammah, then the rest of the seven sons, but Samuel could not find the son of Jesse whom the Lord had chosen. He knew there had to be one more. Then Jesse told Samuel that his youngest son was out tending the sheep. So Samuel had Jesse call for him, "Now he was ruddy, with beautiful eyes and a handsome appearance. And the LORD said, 'Arise, anoint him; for this is he'" (1 Samuel 16:12).

Heart vision, regardless of your age, is when you love God with everything you have, and your vision shifts from the eyes to the heart.

When God told Samuel to anoint David, Samuel understood there was something very special about this boy-man whom God chose to be the next king. David had 20/20 heart vision. Heart vision, regardless of your age, is when you love God with everything you have, and your vision shifts from the eyes to the heart. On the spot, when Samuel heard God's command, he took the oil from his horn and anointed David as the new king of Israel. Those drops of oil shimmered with the Light as the spiritual seed traveled through the faith-family tree.

A good number of years passed from when David was anointed to when he actually became the king of Israel. As king, his leadership would preserve the chosen nation. In the meantime, David had to remember that this was just the beginning of his God-story. There would be struggles, but God would continue to take him where God wanted him to go.

Hear and Obey

David's deep faith developed as a young boy in his Israelite home where he learned about our steadfast God. As a boy, he would have recited the Shema (prayer) daily, "Hear O Israel, the LORD our God, the LORD is One" in order to remind himself of God's oneness, how He belonged to God, and to show his commitment to God.

Shema Israel, Adonai Elohenu, Adonai Echad
(Deuteronomy 6:4).

When I first asked my grandfather about the Shema, his eyes welled up with tears. I knew he loved passing his legacy to me, so in my affection for him, I often saved up questions for him. He explained to me that to *shema* means more than just "to hear." It means to obey, or take action. It is said two to three times a day, always when the sun comes up and at dusk. The custom of some Jewish people is to say it before going to bed as well.

When the seed falls on the nutrient-rich soil, or an ever-ready heart, one will *shema* — hear and obey. The nutrient-rich soil has "ears to hear."

> 'Hear, O Israel: the Lord our God, the Lord is one. Love the Lord your God with all your heart and with all your soul and with all your mind and with all your strength.' The second is this: 'Love your neighbor as yourself.' There is no commandment greater than these (Mark 12:29-31 NIV).

The importance of oneness pressed hard from God's heart into the hearts of His people. When His people understood the depth of His love for them, and chose to follow Him, they became one. When we understand the depth of the Father's love for us, and choose to follow Him, we become one.

Most of us long for consistency in our lives. As a mom, I have loved every stage of my children's lives. Some stages were more difficult than others, but in the middle of each stage I would long for time to freeze. Then they would grow into the next stage, I would accept the change again, it would be so good, I would want time to freeze, and then they would grow again! Change is certain. Christ is constant.

Change is certain.
Christ is constant.

Our bodies are constantly changing (physically and emotionally) as we age, and we must take care of them. Our children need attention and nourishment, so we take care of them. Our gardens need weeding and pruning, and we must take care of them. Our lawn continues to grow, and we must take care of it. Our roots show gray or change color, and we need to maintain them! Just as soon as the laundry basket is empty, it seems to fill right back up again! Our lives at times feel overwhelmed with "upkeep"!

And our human hearts long to hold onto a love that never fails.

Our human hearts long to
hold onto a love that never fails.

Consistency Creates Intimacy

David knew God was always present — even when he could not see God with his physical eyes. David's battle with Goliath was won by his heavenly perspective. As a shepherd, David warded off lions, bears, and wolves from his sheep. He grew up using a stick and stones as weapons, so when it was time to ward off the massive Philistine, he knew with a quiet confidence that God had prepared him.

David knew God and God knew David. The Hebrew word *yada* means to be known on a personal level.[2] It means to be intimately acquainted with someone. David describes his intimate relationship with the Lord later on in his life when he scribed the words of Psalm 139:

> O Lord, You have searched me and known me. You know when I sit down and when I rise up; You understand my thought from afar. You scrutinize my path and my lying down, and are intimately acquainted with all my ways (Psalm 139:1-3).

Yada is used to describe the type of closeness in the sexual relationship between husband and wife, man and woman. Marriage is the closest relationship here on earth that can be compared to the closeness of knowing God. This oneness is the intimacy that you find from spending time with someone, in someone's presence, learning about his heart and his pure love for you. The one you *yada* is someone whom you know well and is there for you in the good times and in the bad times.

David had his fair share of bad times and was often pursued by his enemies. He had to hide for his life, and in the midst of his despair, when he felt his lowest, he turned to God and gave God praise. When David feigned madness before Abimelech, the King of Gath, he said, "I will bless the LORD at all times; His praise shall continually be in my mouth" (Psalm 34:1).

Centuries later, Paul referred back to David's example when he wrote to the Philippians, "Rejoice in the Lord always; again I will say, rejoice!" (Philippians 4:4). Always. At all times. Sometimes I can honestly say that I do not feel like rejoicing. Rejoicing is difficult when I am busy, tired of keeping up with everything, sick, or sad. Rejoicing is hard when I forget to pay a bill, or when I get into an argument with my child, and he tells me that I've ruined his morning.

Rejoicing when our hearts are heavy is hard. When we are tempted to despair, what is called for is a "sacrifice" of praise (Hebrews 13:15).

God doesn't say that our trials are good. He does not say to idolize the trials. No. Rather, He says to rejoice always, even through our trials, because it's when our trials are the most difficult that we look towards Him, grab for Him, come to know Him, and find rest in Him. We rest in God when our hearts understand God's sovereignty, and then we strive to follow Him. We understand that He is our God through the good and the bad and in Him we are one: *Shema Israel, Adonai Elohenu, Adonai Echad* (Deuteronomy 6:4).

If we focus on the Savior instead of ourselves, we can rejoice in the truth that Jesus overcame death, and so will we one day. Since Jesus is alive, He is our Living Hope. The cross symbolizes victory as it shines the Light into the darkness of our trials. The cross becomes our deadly weapon against despair. We allow His life to bolster hope. We trust in the miracle that He is alive!

> And not only this, but we also exult in our tribulations, knowing that tribulation brings about perseverance; and perseverance, proven character; and proven character, hope; and hope does not disappoint, because the love of God has been poured out within our hearts through the Holy Spirit who was given to us (Romans 5:3-5).

David knew despair, but his hope came from being in the presence of God. When he was away from God, when his heart was down, he set the example for us to follow. He worshipped. He knew what it was like to be in the wilderness — not only physically, but spiritually. How did he worship with an empty heart? In the lowest of times, he fell on his face and worshipped God. When David felt as though he was outside of the presence of God, David longed again to be inside of the presence of God, "Why are you in despair, O my soul? And why have you become disturbed within me? Hope in God, for I shall again praise Him for the help of His presence" (Psalm 42:5).

> In David's Jewish home, he would have said the Shema.
> In Jesus' Jewish home, he would have said the Shema.

Holocaust survivor, Viktor Frankl, wrote in his book *Man's Search for Meaning* about the deepest experience he had in the concentration camp. Even though God took Him to the depths of despair, he continued to give encouragement and hope to the other prisoners within the camp, as he helped them see their value and find the meaning of life. Frankl states, "A man who becomes conscious of the responsibility he bears toward a human being who affectionately waits for him, or to an unfinished work, will never be able to throw away his life."[3] Frankl lived for his family; then he found out they passed away. He lived for the manuscript of his first book, which was hidden in his original coat that he had to hand over when he arrived to Auschwitz. Neither his family, nor the manuscript survived the Holocaust. However, in the rags from an inmate who was placed in the gas chamber, which he was given to wear, he found that, "instead of my manuscript, I found in a pocket of the newly acquired coat one single page torn out of a Hebrew prayer book, containing the most important Jewish prayer, *Shema Yisrael.*"

He reflected, "How should I have interpreted such a 'coincidence' other than as a challenge to live my thoughts instead of merely putting them on paper?"[4]

Shema Israel, Adonai Elohenu, Adonai Echad (Deuteronomy 6:4). Once again in English this means: "Hear Israel, the Lord our God, the Lord our God is one." The Shema helps us remember who we are, who God is, and how we are one together.

God doesn't only want us to hear Him, but then He wants us to follow Him.

Andrew Murray says this about being in the presence of God:

> The precious blood of Christ has opened the way for the believer into God's presence, and intimacy with Him is a deep, spiritual reality...In intimacy with God, he is able to hear the softest whispers of the Holy Spirit. He learns to understand the slightest sign of his Father's will and to follow it. His strength continually increases, for God is his strength and God is ever with him. ~Andrew Murray, *The Practice of God's Presence: Cleansed by the Blood to Serve the Living God* [5]

Our hearts long to have oneness. In marriage, the concept of oneness begins immediately, "For this reason a man shall leave his father and his mother, and be joined to his wife; and they shall become one flesh" (Genesis 2:24). Husband and wife know each other intimately, and the intimacy found in marriage is an example of the intimacy, or oneness, we have in God.

How do we enter into the presence of God? How do we get to the place where our hearts are full and our souls are at rest? We set our eyes on Him — and we praise Him. We let go of yesterday and embrace today. Praise, confess, give thanks, and praise again. Worship begins with praise and then confession. Confession opens the door to worship. Confession brings healing to soul wounds. When we receive forgiveness, we thank Him. As we thank Him, we receive even more grace for the trials we face. We gain confidence to approach the throne of God with our needs. We can praise Him more, and the power of worship lifts us "from glory to glory" (2 Corinthians 3:18). Once again, we shift our perspective from self to Savior, and He transforms our thoughts and captures our imaginations.

Can we truly lift up our hearts if they are heavily burdened down? Remember, God does not tolerate sin in His presence. If the object of worship is the face of a righteous God, we need to let go of our iniquities in order to be in His presence.

God, I want to be in Your presence and see Your face. Open the eyes of my heart, Lord. May I lay my burdens down at the foot of the cross.

He Knows

God promised Joshua He would be with him and that Joshua would win the battles. However, they were permitted only to conquer; they were banned from plundering the inhabitants of the lands they conquered. "But the sons of Israel acted unfaithfully in regard to the things under the ban, for Achan … from the tribe of Judah, took some of the things under the ban, therefore the anger of the LORD burned against the sons of Israel" (Joshua 7:1).

When Joshua lost the battle at Ai, he pleaded with God and asked God what he did. God told Joshua that it was not what he did, but what one of his men did. God sees all and knows all. Apparently, Achan did not fully understand God's omniscience. Achan had hidden spoil from the battle — gold, silver, and a beautiful robe in the ground inside his tent. So Joshua implored Achan to reveal his secret. "Then Joshua said to Achan, 'My son, I implore you, give glory to the LORD, the God of Israel, and give praise to Him; and tell me now what you have done. Do not hide it from me" (Joshua 7:19). If God was not watching, Achan could have gotten away with his secret loot.

But God knew, and there were consequences.

Sin fractures and shatters the soul. ~ John Ortberg, *Soul Keeping*[6]

Keep in mind, you cannot bring glory to the LORD if you are hiding something from Him in your heart. There are no hiding spaces from God. He knows your heart — every nook and cranny of it, "But as for me, I shall walk in my integrity; redeem me, and be gracious to me" (Psalm 26:11). Our souls are a part of our bodies and when sin is present, everything else within us is affected.

When our hearts are pure, we see the world from a heavenly perspective. "God blesses those whose hearts are pure, for they will see God" (Matthew 5:8 NLT). How do we know? We trust that God keeps His promises. God can see the big picture — we cannot. Understanding comes from knowing He has a purpose for what is going on in our lives. Our God is a covenant-keeping God. When our vision shifts from self to Savior, our perspective shifts from what we can see with our eyes to what we know in our hearts. God gives us a heavenly perspective, which is 20/20 heart vision. We would never want to live in sin, hiding from His sweet presence.

How my eyes see, perspective, is my key to enter into His gates. I can only do so with thanksgiving. If my inner eye has God seeping up through all things, then can't I give thanks for anything? And if I can give thanks for the good things, the hard things, the absolute everything, I can enter the gates to glory. Living in His presence is fullness of joy — and seeing shows the way in. Ann Voskamp, *One Thousand Gifts: A Dare to Live Fully Right Where You Are*[7]

If I do not understand, I cannot see the way in. If I cannot see, I cannot enter into intimacy with God. Intimacy comes from understanding, and understanding comes from knowing the depth and the root of a Father's love. Consistency creates intimacy. Jesus, our constant Friend, enables us to enjoy this intimacy from now into eternity.

Intimacy creates oneness and allows for our souls to sing,

Shema Israel, Adonai Elohenu, Adonai Echad (Deuteronomy 6:4).

The Olive Tree: Grafted

Two come together permanently when the graft union occurs so they will continue to grow as one. A scion, or new, separate tree, is grafted into the original rootstock. The scion can't survive without the durability that comes from the rootstock, and the rootstock cannot grow to produce fruit without the scion. Normally, grafting occurs by inserting a good scion into a wild stock.

Intimacy comes from understanding,
and understanding comes from knowing
the depth and the root of a Father's love.

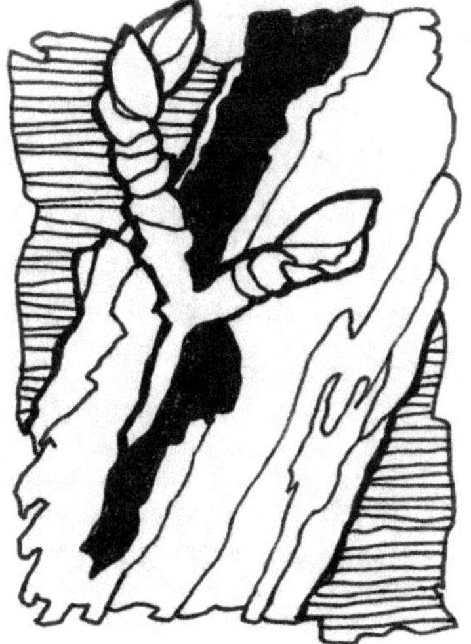

Contrary to normal practice, in the New Testament, Paul says that the wild olive was grafted into a cultivated stock (Romans 11:24).[8] Only by God's grace can the grafting occur in the reverse way Paul describes!

Believers are grafted into the original faith-family tree. Just as an olive tree cannot produce edible fruit without being grafted, Jews and Gentiles are grafted together as one in order to thrive and produce fruit.

Intimacy is the opposite of enmity (Genesis 3:14). When hope is born in the hearts of the believers the two become one in Him. We are one body of believers!

 *Two come together permanently when the graft union occurs so they will continue to grow as one.*

Together we are brothers and sisters in Christ as one body of believers, "There is neither Jew nor Gentile, neither slave nor free, nor is there male and female, for you are all one in Christ Jesus. If you belong to Christ, then you are Abraham's seed, and heirs according to the promise" (Galatians 3:28-29 NIV). The sturdy roots support and anchor the tree. Wild, distracting, and unfruitful branches are broken off, or pruned. United, you and I comprise the grafted olive tree, and our roots run deep to the beginning of time. We are grafted and growing together as one!

If the part of the dough offered as first fruits is holy, then the whole batch is holy; if the root is holy, so are the branches. If some of the branches have been broken off, and you, though a wild olive shoot, have been grafted in among the others and now share in the nourishing sap from the olive root, do not consider yourself to be superior to those other branches. If you do, consider this: You do not support the root, but the root supports you. You will say then, 'Branches were broken off so that I could be grafted in.' Granted. But they were broken off because of unbelief, and you stand by faith. Do not be arrogant, but tremble. For if God did not spare the natural branches, he will not spare you either (Romans 11:16-21 NIV).

The great holy root supports and gives new life to ALL believers who choose to follow God. We are eternally grafted together as one into the holy tree because of our belief in the Father, Son, and Holy Spirit. As the branches spread up and out, our roots grow deep. You may be aware of one or two generations before your own, but when you are grafted into God's family, you can see the fingerprints of His careful cultivation of the roots of your faith-family tree. This picture of a strong, mature olive tree represents our faith-family tree that traces back from the beginning of time to today.

By the death of His Son, His resurrection, and our belief in Him, our bodies are transformed into bodies that will never die. "For what the Law could not do, weak as it was through the flesh, God did: sending His own Son in the likeness of sinful flesh and as an offering for sin, He condemned sin in the flesh, so that the requirement of the Law might be fulfilled in us, who do not walk according to the flesh but according to the Spirit" (Romans 8:3-4).

Now we walk according to the Spirit, as children graciously adopted by the Lord, and only by His grace is there, "a remnant according to God's gracious choice. But if it is by grace, it is no longer on the basis of works, otherwise grace is no longer grace" (Romans 11:5-6). We are grafted together through the cross by His grace. Grafting produces consistency, intimacy, and oneness. As brothers and sisters in Christ, we can praise the Lord for His relentless pursuit of each one of us!

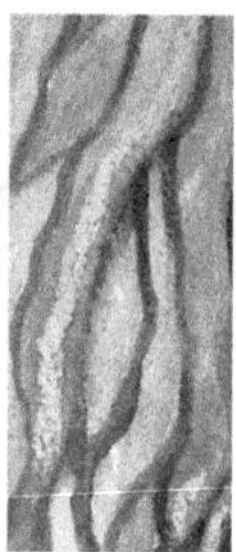

TREASURE, PRAYER, AND REFLECTION

Scripture Treasure

"Hear, O Israel! The LORD is our God, the LORD is one!" (Deuteronomy 6:4).

Praying God's Promises

Heavenly Father,

I praise You for Your consistency. You have always loved me and pursued me. I praise You for giving me the opportunity to be consistent with You. Consistency creates intimacy, and intimacy creates oneness. I praise You for giving me the confidence to let go of yesterday and cling to You today and into tomorrow. Thank You for being my Savior, my Redeemer, my Restorer, my Provider… the Lover of my soul. Thank You for grafting me into Your forever faith-family tree. I praise You.

In Your precious name, Jesus, I pray,
Amen

Spiritual Discipline: *Worship*

Worship includes praising, confessing, and thanksgiving! It begins with praising God for who He is and what He is doing in our lives. Then we confess mistakes, or sins, that we are aware of, and even the ones we are not aware of. Confession brings healing to soul wounds. His forgiveness comes from the mountains of grace He heaps upon us, and then we thank Him! It's at this moment that we gain the confidence we need to approach the throne of God.

We may worship God with praise music, but a spiritual act of worship also includes the way we keep our homes, love our spouses, and serve our children. We may worship God by giving in creative ways above and beyond our tithing. To worship means that we are in the continuous presence of God, and that is how we come to know Him more.

Deep Roots Reflection
Old Testament Word: *yada* (Hebrew)
to know, learn to know, to perceive[9]

When you know someone in an intimate way, you *yada* him. You can recognize him for who he really is, in a deep, caring, and understanding way. You see past the façade and straight into his heart. The intimate relationship between husband and wife here on earth represents the intimate relationship one has with the Heavenly Father.

Look up the following verses and write them in the spaces provided. Then take time to answer the following questions.

Psalm 139:1 ~

____

____

____

____

He knows you. What part of your life are you still trying to keep from Him? How does it feel to be intimately known by the One who loves you completely?

____

____

____

Romans 8:27 ~

____

____

____

____

He searches our hearts and intercedes for us. He desires you and He wants to see you succeed. How does this help you see your life today?

____

____

____

____

If He already knows, then why is it so hard for us to confess? Confession is important. Harboring sin and guilt weighs your heart down and keeps you in a state of pride instead of in a state of repentance. Confess your sins to God and let Him clean your heart. Nail your sins to the cross – that is why Jesus came. "God blesses those whose hearts are pure, for they will see God" (Matthew 5:8 NLT). You may use this space to write down the sins you want to place on the cross.

____

____

____

____

> Then Joshua said to Achan, "My son, I implore you, give glory to the LORD, the God of Israel, and give praise to Him; and tell me now what you have done. Do not hide it from me (Joshua 7:19).

God is omnipotent, omnipresent, and omniscient. He knows. If there is a sin hiding in your heart, He already knows about it. You might as well let it go, and let Him carry it for you. You will not be able to move forward in your relationship with Him until you let it go. Is there anything else in your life that you need to let go of?

____

____

____

____

Confessing your sin lets you cast the 20-pound weight off of your back and lets you walk confidently and freely in Christ, the Lover of your soul, who is carrying it for you. He already knows. When you confess, you acknowledge that He already knows and you allow for healing to begin. In light of what you just wrote down that you need to throw off, and referring back to chapter two's responses, what is God calling you to do today?

____

____

____

____

____

____

Praising God in the good times is easy. "I will bless the LORD at all times; His praise shall continually be in my mouth" (Psalm 34:1). Are you able to praise Him during the storms of life as well as when the blessings come? Now that you have acknowleged the sins you are going to throw off in order to walk confidently in your calling, take some time to praise Him now. Write down words of adoration to your Creator, Father, and Lover of your soul. When the storms of life come, return to this place.
Remember these words.
You have been set free!

____

____

____

____

____

____

____

The LORD's loving kindnesses indeed never cease, For His compassions never fail. They are new every morning; Great is Your faithfulness (Lamentations 3:22-23).

When we commit to follow Christ it does not mean that life will be sunny and easy all of the time. There will be times when we feel let down, and there will be times when we let others down. One truth we can hide in our hearts is this: "Regardless of the circumstances, the Son is always shining." How has God been compassionate towards you?

____

____

____

____

____

____

____

Listen, Understand, and Obey

Do you pray for your children and your family as soon as you rise? Do you read Scripture together at breakfast? Do you pray over your children as you drop them off in the car line? Do you say prayers together at night? Do you use real life experiences to explain a Christian worldview? Do you take your children to church to worship with others?

Teach the Word to your children, so that the legacy of faith may be passed down to the next generation. The Shema is taught to and recited by every Hebrew child, from the youngest age: *Shema Israel, Adonai Elohenu, Adonai Echad* (Deuteronomy 6:4).

Passing down the legacy of your faith is your responsibility.

> You must arrange your days so that you are experiencing deep contentment, joy, and confidence in your everyday life with God. ~ Dallas Willard [10]

How will you rearrange your life today, so you may find contentment, joy, and confidence in God? When your soul finds rest in God, you are able to understand who He is and His will for your life. Then, you may pass down the legacy of your faith to your children. You cannot expect others to do it for you. As a parent who has been grafted into the forever faith-family tree, this is part of your responsibility, as well as a great privilege!

List three things you do (or you will do) to help your children's hearts see the legacy.

____

____

____

____

____

____

____

____

Beautiful Legacy Reminder

Consistency produces intimacy with God. Listen for Him, acknowledge Him, and rest in Him. Intimacy comes from praise, confession, thanksgiving, supplication, and praise again. Just like David, you are anointed by the Word, through the Savior, to be intimate with God.

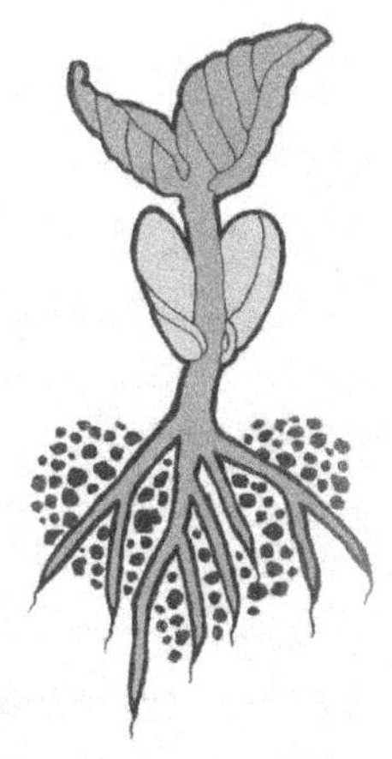

CHAPTER SIX
Redeemed

*The heart of the gospel is redemption,
and the essence of redemption
is the substitutionary sacrifice of Christ.*
~ C.H. Spurgeon[1]

While we were packing up our house and preparing to move away from Florida, my husband found his stash of gift cards. For years our family gave him gift cards to his favorite store, Bass Pro Shops, but he never used them. Instead, he saved them in one big pile in his dresser. He had so many gift cards that he was able to cash them all in at once for a fishing kayak! He walked out of the store with what felt like a free boat!

Redeeming the value of a gift card is a treat, since the price for the item has already been paid. We have the ability to redeem the free gift, or in other words, to buy it back, at any time. However, gift cards are only used to redeem temporary items.

While temporary items are good for the moment, they fade with time. Our Heavenly Father paid the eternal price to give us His eternal gift, and by that price, He redeemed mankind to have a shining future in heaven with Him.

God's Eternal Gift

God loved His chosen nation; however, they were caught in an ongoing cycle: worship, rebel, repent, and repeat. After 400 years, this greatest gift, Jesus, was given to the world right in the middle of the greatest story. His presence split time. This heaven-sent soul was fully God and fully man.

As a young child, Jesus grew up under the nourishment and guidance of his Jewish mother and father. He no doubt learned the Shema, as all Jewish children do, and even though He knew all, Jesus, as God Himself, yet observed and learned, then taught.

He was a 30-year-old man before he began his teaching ministry. As God in human form, reflecting the image of His father, Jesus taught the people how to live with mercy, respect, and goodness. "But when the fullness of time came, God sent forth His Son, born of a woman, born under the Law, so that He might redeem those who were under the Law, that we might receive adoption as sons" (Galatians 4:4-5).

All of mankind was separated from God as a result of Adam and Eve's sin, "Therefore, just as through one man sin entered into the world, and death through sin, and so death spread to all men, because all sinned" (Romans 5:12). God forgave Adam and Eve; however, they lived the rest of their lives with the consequences of their sin. They were banished from the beautiful Garden of Eden to live in bondage to sin. Sin is legalistic, prideful, and controlling. Sin whispers to your heart and to your soul that you're not good enough. Sin compares, and sin drives unhealthy competition. In this world, we all live in the consequence of sin. But from the moment of the curse, God offered hope in the form of grace and forgiveness!

Our individual lives are comprised of a multitude of backgrounds and cultures, and we have our own unique stories. Based on what we can see in the present day, it's very easy to hold a measuring stick up to our past. People judge stories. We compare our pasts to see whose was the worst, or whose was the best. We all have issues, and everyone one of us has struggled with strongholds — some worse than others. Regardless of particulars, all of our stories originated with the same original sin; therefore, we all need a Savior.

Through His grace, God sent His Son to redeem, or buy back,

mankind from the same original sin, which had resulted in spiritual death: "... but from the tree of the knowledge of good and evil you shall not eat, for in the day that you eat from it you will surely die" (Genesis 2:17).

Regardless of your background, culture, social status, or gender — God sent His Son to save you. The blood of Christ redeems both Jews and Gentiles. When we believe, His blood covers our sin from yesterday, today, and tomorrow, and we become God's sons and daughters. He adopts us and loves us as His own. God becomes our adoptive Father, "you have received a spirit of adoption as sons by which we cry out, 'Abba! Father!'" (Romans 8:15b).

The Source of eternal life — redemption —
is a Person, not a program, which means it cannot
be purchased with money, and no one can boast
of earning or deserving it.

Purchased by the Blood

Christ came to redeem the relationship that was broken in the fall. God offered redemption by the blood of His Son on the cross, once and for all, so that we may come to Him and live in relationship with Him again. "He did not enter by means of the blood of goats and calves; but he entered the Most Holy Place once for all by his own blood, thus obtaining eternal redemption" (Hebrews 9:12 NIV). The Source of eternal life — redemption — is a Person, not a program, which means it cannot be purchased with money, and no one can boast of earning or deserving it. "For by grace you have been saved through faith; and that not of yourselves, it is the gift of God; not as a result of works, so that no one may boast" (Ephesians 2:8-9). Faith comes from God, and grace is the gift of God.

Just as in the Passover story the Israelites were delivered out of Egyptian bondage by the blood of a lamb, you and I are delivered out of the bondage of sin by the blood of the Lamb, "... knowing that you were not redeemed with perishable things like silver or gold from your futile way of life inherited from your forefathers, but with precious blood, as of a lamb unblemished and spotless, the blood of Christ" (1 Peter 1:18-19).

The blood of Christ delivers us. The blood of Christ justifies us — makes us righteous —before the King of Kings. The blood of Christ covers our sins from yesterday, today, and tomorrow.

> In reality, salvation was bought not by Jesus' fist, but by His nail-pierced hands; not by muscle but by love; not by vengeance, but by forgiveness; not by force, but by sacrifice. Jesus Christ our Lord surrendered in order that He might win; He destroyed His enemies by dying for them and conquered death by allowing death to conquer Him. A.W. Tozer, *Preparing for Jesus' Return: Daily Live the Blessed Hope* [2]

The greatest sacrificial gift of all time is the greatest victory of all time. Jesus won. His death gives us life. The depth of the Father's love is hardly comprehensible to a human parent. Our parental instincts would never allow us to sacrifice our own children. But God's love was so deep, He allowed His only Son to die. God let His Son die for you, for me, for our children, and for our children's children, because He made a promise in the very beginning of time.

In our intimacy with God, we remember God's promises to us, God's love for us, and God's accomplishments through us.

> The LORD did not set his affection on you and choose you because you were more numerous than other peoples, for you were the fewest of all peoples. But it was because the LORD loved you and kept the oath he swore to your ancestors that he brought you out with a mighty hand and redeemed you from the land of slavery, from the power of Pharaoh king of Egypt (Deuteronomy 7:7-8 NIV).

God chose the small nation of Israel so that His power could be seen working within them. It is only by His power that such great accomplishments could take place. The Israelite nation was not massive in number or strength. But they had the strength of the Lord with them, with which nobody could compete. As stated in Chapter Five, consistency creates intimacy. Intimacy produces oneness.

In our intimacy with God, we remember God's promises to us, God's love for us, and God's accomplishments through us.

When we lack intimacy with God, we forget His promises, and anxiety creeps into life. Forgetting God's promises produces destructive consequences. Several prophets who spoke to the kings who reigned after King David mentioned this. Each prophet reminded the Israelites: If you obey God you will be protected; however, if you disobey God, you will have consequences. Turn back to God!

Do you not know? Have you not heard? The Everlasting God, the LORD, the Creator of the ends of the earth does not become weary or tired. His understanding is inscrutable. He gives strength to the weary, and to him who lacks might he increases power. Though youths grow weary and tired, and vigorous young men stumble badly, yet those who wait for the LORD will gain new strength; they will mount up with wings like eagles, they will run and not get tired, they will walk and not become weary (Isaiah 40:28-31).

Isaiah reminds the nation of Israel of God's sovereignty. He says to them, "How many times do I have to tell you? God does not have a beginning or an end. He is the Creator, which means that He made you with a purpose in mind. He never gets tired. Look to Him, and He will give you strength when you are weary."

When we wait for God, we allow God to move and tackle our problems by the power of the Holy Spirit. "Jesus answered, 'Very truly I tell you, no one can enter the kingdom of God unless they are born of water and the Spirit. Flesh gives birth to flesh, but the Spirit gives birth to spirit'" (John 3:5-6 NIV). When we are born of the Spirit, the Spirit moves on our behalf.

God's redemptive love comes from the death and resurrection of His Son. A life needed to be shed in order for the lives to be saved.

The blood of His Son was shed to cover our sins (which is atonement) and to make us righteous. Only a righteous person may enter the presence of the righteous God. From the moment we believe, the blood covers us. When God looks at us, He no longer sees failure, disobedience, anger, or strife. Instead, He looks at those who believe, and He sees the blood of His Son.

> *This new heart contains the gift*
> *of the indwelling of the Holy Spirit,*
> *who causes our wants and desires to*
> *shift from desiring the world to desiring God.*

Redemption comes from God by way of the blood of the Lamb. The imperishable seed, nourished by the washing of the Word, creates new life in us and gives us a new heart — a heart completely cultivated and pruned by the Holy Spirit. This new heart contains the gift of the indwelling of the Holy Spirit, who causes our wants and desires to shift from desiring the world to desiring God.

A Heart Transplant

God gives you a new heart: "And I will give you a new heart, and I will put a new spirit in you. I will take out your stony, stubborn heart and give you a tender, responsive heart. And I will put my Spirit in you …" (Ezekiel 36:26-27a, NLT).

I recently watched an older movie with my son about a teenage boy who was sick and in need of a heart transplant. Perhaps you have seen it, too; it's unforgettable, and it's an apt illustration for our situation without Christ. The storyline of the movie begins by presenting the situation of the sick boy. If the sick boy does not receive a new heart, he will most certainly die. The conflict and tension within the story is that to get another heart, there will have to be a donor. Unfortunately, another teenager is killed in a car accident. He dies, but his heart is still in good condition. The heart of the boy from the accident is promptly harvested and transplanted into the sick child's body. The sick child gets a completely new heart, which makes him alive and well.

My "mama's heart" can still picture the end of the movie. The mother of the child who died visited the family of the child who received her son's heart. When the mom arrived, she was given a stethoscope, so she could hear her son's heart beat. She listened, and she shed tears of grief — and joy. The death of her son gave this other, precious teenager new life.

The seed of Christ cannot grow in a heart of stone. When the seed is planted, a heart transplant occurs. This transplant is instant, and it is comprehensive in nature: Now you have a tender heart responsive to the Spirit in you. From the moment of our transplant, God lives in us and works through us.

When God gives us a new heart, it comes with new desires created from a new perspective from which the heart views the world. Our new heart sees people as God sees people, wanting no one to perish, but all to return to Him. Our new perspective allows for us to see God's involvement in all aspects of our lives. We begin to understand that He loves us, every part of us, even the smallest details of our lives.

Our new heart makes us uncomfortable in situations that never bothered us before, and we notice things about our friends that we never noticed before. Our eyes are opened to the sin with which we once tried to fill ourselves. We have become grafted into the faith-family tree, and new life flows in us.

Christ leads us. Christ redeems us. Christ unites us as one, and then we are filled with the Holy Spirit so that we may thrive as God produces fruit through us.

The Olive Tree: *The Sap*

At the moment an individual believes, the gift of the Holy Spirit is imparted. When the grafting occurs, a new tree grows and the life-giving sap emerges. The life-giving sap, otherwise known as the Holy Spirit, was not accessible to the believer until the new covenant was established through the death and resurrection of Jesus Christ.

The death of God's Son allows for both Jew and Gentile to enter into God's covenant and His holy presence—and also made a way for the Holy Spirit to dwell within every believer. "Christ redeemed us from the curse of the Law, having become a curse for us — for it is written, 'CURSED IS EVERYONE WHO HANGS ON A TREE' — in order that in Christ Jesus the blessing of Abraham might come to the Gentiles, so that we would receive the promise of the Spirit through faith" (Galatians 3:13-14).

When Jesus taught, He reminded people of God's love, mercy, and grace, but the Master Teacher did not stay here with us. Christ redeemed us from the covenant of the law that mankind could not keep, and the blessing came through Him to all. Then God sent mankind the Helper to live in us, "But I tell you the truth, it is to your advantage that I go away; for if I do not go away, the Helper will not come to you; but if I go, I will send Him to you" (John 16:7).

In the olive tree, the sap carries the nutrients it needs to grow, survive, thrive, and bear fruit. It finds the nutrients and water and then delivers them to specific locations within the tree where they are needed. *The sap seeks out the water and draws it in to give life to the tree.*

The Holy Spirit is constantly seeking out connection with our Heavenly Father to help the believer grow, survive, thrive, and bear fruit. From the moment I placed my trust in Christ, the Holy Spirit within me sought nourishment from God's Word wherever I could find it: church, online ministries, books, and Christian friends.

Notice that Romans 11:17 calls the rootstock the "rich root." Our faith-family tree's roots are deep, and not only that, they are rich — rich in the DNA and presence of the living God in whose image we are created. The roots are also rich in life-giving sustenance that keeps the branches green. They are rich in containing evidence of an ancient Biblical heritage. Through those roots, we who compose the faith-family tree are also rich in God's love, His strength, His favor, and the ancestry we have by being adopted into His bloodline. I am a new creation - adopted and loved as God's chosen daughter, and as my faith grows, I thrive, so that God's spiritual legacy can be passed down to the next generation through me.

When you believe, you are connected to the life-giving sap of the Holy Spirit who nourished the saints of all the ages, from Christian leaders of today, to D.L. Moody, John Wesley, the Moravians, the great thinkers of the Enlightenment and further back to John Calvin and Martin Luther during the Reformation, through saints and martyrs of the Dark Ages, to the early apostles, back through the Old Testament prophets, kings, judges, to the Hebrews under Moses and Joshua, to the patriarchs, Abraham, Isaac and Jacob, all the way back to Adam and Eve!

We have riches of wisdom, tradition, faith, strength, and all the spiritual blessings that come through living as the next generation in the family tree! We were raised up for such a time as this. We have inherited spiritual riches in our roots – isn't that worth getting excited about?

TREASURE, PRAYER, AND REFLECTION

Scripture Treasure

"To redeem them that were under the law, that we might receive adoption of sons" (Galatians 4:5 KJV).

Praying God's Promises

Heavenly Father,

I praise You for the gift of Your Son whom You gave freely to all who believe. My freedom was bought with the price of His blood. The blood sacrifice You paid, dear Jesus, was once and for all. It redeems me for eternity since I am adopted as God's child. I praise You for bringing Jews and Gentiles together as one body of believers in You. I am grateful for my sisters and brothers in Christ. I am grateful for my new heart, which beats for You — all for Your splendor.

In Your precious name, Jesus, I pray,
Amen

Spiritual Discipline: *Serve*

"Beloved, let us love one another, for love is from God" (1 John 4:7a). Take a moment and read 1 John 4:7-21. When we understand the depth of God's redeeming love, we can't help but let Him use us to love others. Serving involves acts of kindness and doing things that most people don't like to do, such as cleaning up certain areas in the home or making special meals even if you don't enjoy eating them!

Sharing the gospel, or evangelism, may also be a form of serving, as well as giving. Ask the Lord to reveal to You if there is any area of serving right in front of you, but you have not had eyes to see it. Or if there has been an area your heart longs to serve in but you haven't seen how to do so, ask the Lord to show you. Sometimes being faithful in small service leads to bigger, more exciting tasks.

Deep Roots Reflection
Old Testament Word: *ga'al* (Hebrew)
to redeem, to buy back, to do the part of next of kin, deliver, sometimes requires blood [3]

God paid the ultimate price for your salvation. By the blood of His Son you have been redeemed, or bought back as his adopted child, forever. He calls you His and you have inherited eternal treasures.

Look up the following verses and write them in the spaces provided. Then take time to answer the following questions.

Romans 8:14-15 ~

____

____

____

____

How is this significant in your life?

____

____

____

Galatians 3:26 ~

____

____

____

____

____

How does this impact your life today?

____

____

____

God moves us from tragedy to beauty in His perfect timing.

At the cross you were redeemed. God paid for you with the blood of His own Son, so that He could adopt you and you could live together as One. God bought you back from the original sin of Adam and Eve. When you commit your life to Christ, you become One with other believers. Your family lineage ties into the Hebrew family lineage, which goes all the way back to the beginning of time.

You are also set free from bondage. No longer are you under the covenant of the law. By His blood you are welcomed into a covenant of grace, "For God so loved the world, that He gave His only begotten Son, that whoever believes in Him shall not perish, but have eternal life" (John 3:16).

Jesus was not comfortable on the cross when He redeemed me from the sin I was born with and the sin I created on my own.

My sins of yesterday, today, and tomorrow were nailed to His cross. He took my place, however death did not win. Jesus rose again because the adversary cannot defeat God. Jesus left so we could have God's presence forever in the form of the Holy Spirit. "But I tell you the truth, it is to your advantage that I go away; for if I do not go away, the Helper will not come to you; but if I go, I will send Him to you" (John 16:7).

Once I believed in Him, He took my heart of flesh and gave me His Spirit. Spirit gives birth to Spirit. Nothing can ever separate us from the depth of The Father's everlasting love.

When I think about the tragedy of Christ's crucifixion, I begin to see the beauty of my redemption. Following Him is easy. Nothing He asks me to give up will ever compare to the life He gave up for me.

I will surrender this aspect of my life to Him:

____

____

____

____

Only the Lord can open the eyes of your heart. Your new heart gives you new eyes. How does this help you to see your family, situations, or the world differently?

____

____

____

____

How has your perspective specifically changed in at least one of the areas listed above?

____

____

____

____

The Champion has been born in you and lives in you today.

> Then, when our dying bodies have been
> transformed
> into bodies that will never die,
> this Scripture will be fulfilled:
> 'Death is swallowed up in victory.
> O death, where is your victory?
> O death, where is your sting?'
> For sin is the sting that results in death,
> and the law gives sin its power
> ~ (1 Corinthians 15:54-56 NLT).

Beautiful Legacy Reminder

Death no longer has power over us. I was purchased with the blood of God's Son. The blood of Christ redeems me for eternity. I am a new creation. His heart now beats in me. The eyes of my heart have been opened. Therefore, death has lost its sting!

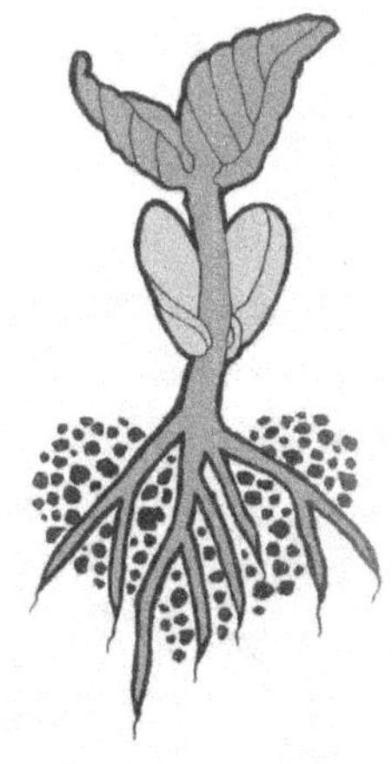

CHAPTER SEVEN

You can drink from all sorts of wells,
but unless the source of your water is the Living Water Himself,
you will never be satisfied.
~ Beth Moore[1]

I was not always a runner. After I had children, I began running to get my body back into shape. I didn't have to drive to a gym, and I could take my babies with me in the jogging stroller. The only thing I had to purchase was a good pair of running shoes! I loved running around the charming, picturesque Florida town where I lived, which smelled of fresh orange blossoms and oak trees. However, in the summertime, it was really, really hot! I always took a bottle (or two) of water with me in order to stay hydrated. If I forgot my water, I returned home parched.

My sister and I found a running program we could do together to prepare us for the Disney marathon. We both lived outside of Orlando, so it seemed as though it was a logical thing for us to do at that time in our lives. The moments we spent together in training were priceless! Our long runs lent themselves to long, private, sisterly conversations. We ran a few shorter races together. Then, for the marathon, my sister made us matching hot-pink sweatshirts with Philippians 4:13 printed on the back: "I can do all things through Him who strengthens me." We were as ready as we could be.

The marathon was on a cold, cold January morning in Orlando. All of the runners were bundled in thick layers over their running clothes. There were a few people who showed up wearing a silver blanket (to keep the body heat in) which they had been given from the Goofy Challenge the day before. The Goofy Challenge allowed for runners to run a crazy amount of miles in two days. I think the "Goofy Challenge" is well-named; it's just plain goofy. Those crazy people ran the half marathon (13.1 miles) the day before, and then they ran the full marathon (26.2 miles) with the rest of us. Just being psyched up for the marathon was exciting enough for me.

As we gathered in the early morning darkness, it was hard to see our way around. But bright overhead lights allowed for the massive amount of runners to find their respective corrals. Everyone around us had cameras in their belts. I had never seen so many cameras at a race before. I wasn't sure what they had them for. Soon, the fireworks went off to announce the start. We didn't take off right away since our corral was so far back, but as soon as we began, the runners surrounding me started shedding their layers of clothes and throwing them all along the roadside (I'm sure those warm clothes made great charitable donations). Once we began running, we realized the cameras were for runners to stop and take pictures with the cast of characters along the way! I was amazed. I couldn't even think about taking pictures with Mickey, Minnie, Donald, or Goofy. I was just trying to start, run, and finish!

Throughout the run, we nourished ourselves with water, bananas, and energy supplements. But around 10:00 a.m., at about mile 25, I hit the wall. If you are a distance runner, then you are familiar with the wall. I was three-fourths of the way through Epcot when my body felt finished. My mind had decided that I could not go any further.

Noticing my struggle, my sister grabbed my hand, and she said, "We're finishing this together!" Another runner came up beside me, handed me a little salt packet and said, "Eat a little bit, and you will make it to the end." I put a little salt on my tongue, and my depleted body pepped up enough to cross the finish line. My body did something amazing, which God created it to do, with Him. My sister and I crossed the line together and raised our hands.

We had finished, thanks to God, each other, a thoughtful fellow runner, and the promise of Philippians 4:13 on our shirts. We cried tears of joy and relief, and breathlessly spoke our gratitude over and over, "Thank You, God!" What an amazing experience we had just survived! Our hearts, minds, and souls overflowed with gratitude.

A Marathon Called Life

Although many people will say they will retire from working at their job one day, we are still running a marathon called life. Our lives are not actually finished until we meet Jesus face to face. Until we meet Jesus, we steadily build spiritual endurance in order to finish the ultimate race. A believer's race is not run in the flesh, but rather by the way of the Holy Spirit. The washing of the Word inspires you, prepares you, and provides endurance. Just as I was not in the Disney marathon alone, as part of God's family, we are also not alone in this challenging race of life.

Not only do we have brothers and sisters in Christ to run with us, the Holy Spirit, too, is with us. God works through the power of the Holy Spirit in each one of us differently. Each one of our struggles is real and they are a part of our stories. God creates the way, and Christ walks through our stories with us as the Champion, otherwise known as the Holy Spirit, who is born in you.

When God is the root of your faith and the source of your strength, you realize there is no life apart from Him.

In Psalm 52:8, David called himself a green olive tree: "But as for me, I am like a green olive tree in the house of God; I trust in the lovingkindness of God forever and ever." The green olive tree is prosperous. As the roots of the olive tree continue to branch out, they bend around rocks and obstacles that get in their way. They constantly seek out nourishment, and when they receive it, they thrive. "I am the vine; you are the branches. If you remain in me and I in you, you will bear much fruit; apart from me you can do nothing" (John 15:5 NIV). When God is the root of your faith and the source of your strength, you realize there is no life apart from Him. He is our constant.

Broken Cisterns

Similar to the prophet Elijah, the prophet Jeremiah also tried to warn the Jewish people they were not walking rightly with God. Jeremiah told God's chosen ones they were worshiping something that would not lead to life, but rather death. "...They have forsaken Me, the fountain of living waters, to hew for themselves cisterns, broken cisterns that can hold no water" (Jeremiah 2:13).

He warned them that God would judge them if they did not turn back to Him. Their broken cisterns would cause them to eventually dry up.

When we neglect to set aside space for God in our lives, our spirits become dry, and peace eludes our souls. When life is moving too fast, and I neglect to set aside space for God in my life, my actions disclose the emptiness in my heart. This is apparent in my life as I tend to become short with my husband and my children, my housework falls behind, the bills pile up, and I begin to compare myself with others instead of seeing how well we complement each other within the body of Christ.

When we neglect to set aside space for God in our lives, our spirits become dry, and peace eludes our souls.

When we turn back to God, He mends our broken cisterns and fills us with gratitude, which leads to contentment in Him. Contentment comes from Christ. When we put God as the first priority in our lives, everything else falls into place, and it comes together for His greater purpose.

The Living Water

Jesus came down to our world to teach us how to live with mercy, respect, and goodness. In John 4:1-42, Jesus was walking from Judea to Galilee. He decided to travel through a town called Samaria. Jesus intentionally sought out a certain woman at the well. Remember, we don't have to be deep in sin to be lost. We are all born with a sin nature that came from Adam and Eve. This woman was guilty of not only her sin nature, but she was living deep in sin.

Jesus knew that once she accepted the good news, she could reach a certain entire people group. He could see the bigger picture, so He knew how the parts needed to come together for the greatest story.

The soul is not satisfied until it meets the Savior.

Jesus sat down at Jacob's well and asked the Samaritan woman for a drink of water. This surprised the Samaritan woman because Jews do not normally speak to Samaritans. Jesus said to her, "If you knew the gift of God and who it is that asks you for a drink, you would have asked him and he would have given you living water" (John 4:10 NIV). Jesus explained to her that everyone who drinks out of Jacob's well will be physically thirsty again.

Jesus was speaking about quenching a different kind of thirst. The living water he spoke of is a spring of water that leads to eternal life. It is the water from the fountain Jeremiah was referring to when he said the Israelites had turned to broken cisterns.

As Jesus and the Samaritan woman continued their conversation, her eyes were opened to the depth of His love for her when He confronted her sin. He told her to go get her husband. She said she didn't have one. That didn't surprise Jesus. He already knew. That is when I picture her jaw dropping. *How does He know?* He saw right through her façade into her heart.

Jesus explained to her that, "God is spirit, and his worshipers must worship in the Spirit and in truth" (John 4:24 NIV). He offered her freedom from her past, instead of the shame of her present. He told her to repent, saying there is a better way. She believed Him. The disciples returned with food for Jesus, but he responded to them that His food is to finish the work of the One who sent Him (John 4:34). Not only with the Samaritan woman, but with the rest of the people in His path, Jesus willingly set aside his own comfort to share the truths of heaven and the way to eternal life.

Jesus presented the living water to nourish her soul and give her the well of eternal life. The soul is not satisfied until it meets the Savior.

The Samaritan woman left and told everyone she knew about the Messiah. She believed, she drank of the living water, and she shared with the people who needed to know. The people came to hear Him because of her story, but they believed because they heard for themselves. They had found the Savior of the world (John 4:39-42). Her enthusiasm was contagious! She believed, and she left to tell everyone she knew!

Is your enthusiasm for your faith contagious? Are you helping to bring others into a relationship with Him? When you find the source of true joy you want to share it with everyone you love and everyone you know!

I am that woman — the woman who turned from filling herself with broken, empty cisterns or things of this world, to filling herself with the endless fountain of living water.

The Samaritan woman shared the good news with all whose hearts were ready to listen. Many people were saved as a result of the humble spirit of this women who placed her trust in God's Son. God bore fruit through her. She reached the exact people group who needed to be reached when she shared the greatest story.

Are you willing to share the story of God's grace with the people whom God has placed where you are?

In His Presence

On earth, Jesus had struggles just like you and I, but He understood that even though the struggles were real, they were only temporary. Just like the woman at the well, Jesus loved people and embraced people in their struggles and through their struggles. He knew His purpose. He offered forgiveness and hope. Complete forgiveness can only occur through the shedding of blood. Jesus was born so that He could die, but he did not stay dead. His death was very similar to a bruise (Genesis 3:15). It was temporary. He died so that we may live.

When His spirit became separated from His lifeless body, the veil in the temple was rent, or torn, from the top down, "And behold, the veil of the temple was torn in two from top to bottom; and the earth shook and the rocks were split" (Matthew 27:51). This gives the believer direct access to God:

> Therefore, brethren, since we have confidence to enter the holy place by the blood of Jesus, by a new and living way which He inaugurated for us through the veil, that is, His flesh, and since we have a great priest over the house of God, let us draw near with a sincere heart in full assurance of faith, having our hearts sprinkled clean from an evil conscience and our bodies washed with pure water (Hebrews 10:19-22).

Jesus' death gives us eternal life and oneness in the healing of our separated relationship. I urge you to draw near to God, boldly approaching Him in His Holy of Holies. Atonement has been taken care of. There, in the house of God, we are strengthened and refreshed with His living water. When we spend time in the presence of God, our hearts are encouraged. Our souls are nourished. It's in the face-to-face encounters that God's Spirit grows from within us.

After Moses received the ten commands from on top of Mt. Sinai, his face shone from speaking with God, and his people were afraid to go near him. Moses told his people to do everything God had told them to do, and then he covered his face with a veil so as not to worry the people. But whenever Moses went in to speak with God, he took the veil off (Exodus 34:29-35).

Moses' face was shining from the inside out. Remember, that's what spending time in God's Word does for us. Spending time in God's presence allows for our souls to shine radiantly from within. Jesus provides a new and living way. He gives us a nourishing, fresh drink when He washes us with the Word: "They looked to Him and were radiant, and their faces will never be ashamed" (Psalm 34:5).

With Great Expectation

Once we believe and turn back to God, our faith story begins and is intimately woven into the greatest story. But the most beautiful part of the story is that we are now rooted to a Living Hope and we live with great expectation for His return:

> All through the Scriptures, we have this panoramic view and glorious expectation of the same Jesus coming again. This harmony of expectation is the beating heart of true Christian experience. It is simply the core of our joy and our delight as believers who long for the return of Jesus.
> ~A.W. Tozer, *Preparing for Jesus' Return*[2]

The Olive Tree: *The Harvest*

Grandparents upon grandparents, generation upon generation, from backgrounds of mixed ideals, races, and cultures, together comprise the branches when the Gentiles and Jews are grafted together as one and fruit grows abundantly from the grafted branches. "For there is no difference between Jew and Gentile – the same Lord is Lord of all and richly blesses all who call on him, for, 'Everyone who calls on the name of the Lord will be saved'" (Romans 10:12-13 NIV).

Independent of each other, the root and the scion cannot grow to become fruitful; however, when they are joined, the sap runs freely, seeking out and delivering nutrients in order for the new tree to thrive and produce fruit. The grafting brings believers together, "that they may all be one" (John 17:21).

When the fruit of the olive tree is hard-pressed, a rich olive oil is produced. As in life, out of pressure arise sheer beauty, sustenance, and radiance. Regardless of the pressure our family tree is exposed to, or the oppression it faces, like the grafted olive tree, it is hardy.

An olive tree with deep roots has a sturdy, gnarled trunk, wide-thick branches, and uniquely beautiful, evergreen silver leaves in the sunshine[3]. In order to help the tree become hardy and fruitful, God prunes the tree of the old growth. When we seek the Lord, listen to Him, and let Him guide us, He prunes our lives of what does not glorify Him.

In hindsight, I can see where God pruned my life of friends, activities, thoughts, or actions that were not fruitful for Him. The strong branches are the channels for the life-giving sap to travel throughout the tree from the root, to the stem, to the blossoms in order to produce the fruit. However, "Every branch in Me that does not bear fruit, He takes away; and every branch that bears fruit, He prunes it so that it may bear more fruit" (John 15:2). The cut-off branches will never have the ability to produce fruit as the grafted branches that abide will. Pruning may be a painful process, but the result is our strength in Christ.

Jesus' audience would have been familiar with the image of fruitfulness from the Old Testament in Psalm 52:8. Again, it says, "But as for me, I am like a green olive tree in the house of God; I trust in the lovingkindness of God forever and ever."

Over time, the olive tree had become a symbol of God's blessings on families who trusted in Him, "Your wife shall be like a fruitful vine within your house, your children like olive plants around your table" (Psalm 128:3). The olive oil was recognized as God's gift and was associated with the outpouring of the Holy Spirit.[4] The new tree, created by the grafting of the branches together to the original rootstock, represents God's forever-faith family tree, which through our belief is where you and I now belong.

We dwell in Him, abide with Him,
and are heavenly rooted in Him
with the goal of producing fruit for Him.

We dwell in Him, abide with Him, and are heavenly rooted in Him with the goal of producing fruit for Him. The heavenly fruit of the grafting is the legacy we leave for our children. Abiding in Christ allows for God to work through us so that He can be revealed in their hearts.

I learned the stories of the New Testament while I was teaching them to my children. (They had no idea we were learning them at the same time!) We listened to every Bible tape or CD for children I could find, so that God's Word would sink deep into our hearts and transform our minds. One of my favorite songs was "This Little Light of Mine." *This little light of mine, I'm gonna let it shine!* God sent His Son to be the "Light of men" (John 1:4) and the "Light of the world" (John 8:12). The words of the song reflected the radiance I felt beaming from within when I spent time in God's Word.

The Master Teacher taught his audience that once we believe, our faith is not something for us to keep to ourselves, "And He was saying to them, 'A lamp is not brought to be put under a basket, is it, or under a bed? Is it not brought to be put on the lampstand? For nothing is hidden, except to be revealed; nor has anything been secret, but that it would come to light. If anyone has ears to hear, let him hear'" (Mark 4:21-23).

God sent Jesus to be the Light in the dark world. *Hide it under a bushel, No! I'm gonna let it shine!* Our job as daughters, wives, parents, friends, workers, neighbors, etc. is to let His heavenly Light shine in every aspect of our lives.

> How, then, can they call on the one they have not believed in? And how can they believe in the one of whom they have not heard? And how can they hear without someone preaching to them? And how can anyone preach unless they are sent? As it is written, 'How beautiful are the feet of those who bring good news!'" (Romans 10:14-16 NIV).

The legacy you share shines beautifully because He is the root and the bright morning star, "I, Jesus, have sent My angel to testify to you these things for the churches. I am the root and the descendant of David, the bright morning star" (Revelation 22:16). When we let His Light shine, the imperishable seed passes from one person to the next, then from one generation to the next, and the amazing power of God grows it abundantly, "So we have the prophetic word made more sure, to which you do well to pay attention as to a lamp shining in a dark place, until the day dawns and the morning star arises in your hearts" (2 Peter 1:19).

It is so exciting to watch Jesus come alive and work in the hearts of those we love, especially if we played a part in planting the imperishable seed in their ready hearts just by creating space for Him to move!

The growth does not depend on man, but solely on God. The mystery of Christ is revealed and it moves in its own mysterious and wonderful way with or without us, but when we let Him move within us, He does amazing things above and beyond what we could have imagined! "Now to Him who is able to do far more abundantly beyond all that we ask or think, according to the power that works within us, to Him be the glory in the church and in Christ Jesus to all generations forever and ever. Amen" (Ephesians 3:20-21).

All we have to do is love Him, follow Him, and create the space for Him to move into our hearts, the hearts of our children, and the hearts of our grandchildren.

Expect great things from God, attempt great things for God.
~William Carey[5]

God's Forever Family

Each one of our unique stories is intricately woven into the greatest story from God's beginning to His perfect ending. Until we meet the Savior, our souls are never satisfied, because we always become Spiritually empty or dry again. But God meets each one of us right where we are. When we place our trust in God's Son (regardless of where we have been or what we have done) our lives are changed, and we receive a new Spiritual DNA from the grafting into His forever-faith family tree. Your legacy begins with the grafting. At that moment, the spiritual connection grafts each person together as one into the family tree, and allows for our roots to run together back to the very beginning of time.

Beloved, you are beautiful because your roots are heavenly. They are rooted in Jesus Christ and you carry a legacy of faith to be passed to the next generation. My hope is for you to understand where the imperishable seed began, and how your life has been forever changed.

Your legacy begins with the grafting. 

May the knowledge of your faith be so full that it can't help but radiate from within, and may you bring God *naches* as you share the depth of His love with your family and the people whom God has placed close to you.

Let us draw near with a true heart that is full of assurance and faith now that we know where our roots began and how God empowers our lives today through our life-giving Savior. May we begin to understand the mystery of Christ: that He was, He is, and He is to come, so that our children may know God and He may lead them into a relationship, prepared for the eternal harvest.

TREASURE, PRAYER, AND REFLECTION

Scripture Treasure
"So now you also receive the blessing God has promised Abraham and His children, sharing in the rich nourishment from the root of God's special olive tree"
(Romans 11:17b, NLT).

Praying God's Promises

Heavenly Father,

I praise You for the deep roots You have given me now that I am adopted into Your family. I praise You for the picture of the olive tree, which symbolizes my deep, rich heritage through the Spirit. When Jews and Gentiles are grafted together as one body of believers, they thrive, and produce fruit for the harvest. Only You could paint such a heavenly rooted, perfect picture. I praise you for forgiveness through the sacrifice of Your own blood. I know I was purchased with a price, and for that I am eternally grateful. Thank You for letting me shine for You. It's because of You that I am radiant.

In Your precious name, dear Jesus, I pray,
Amen

Spiritual Discipline: *Celebrate*
"Rejoice in the Lord always; again I will say, rejoice!" (Philippians 4:4). When we rejoice, we are intentionally looking for joy and sharing it with others. We are celebrating the realization that "Every good thing given and every perfect gift is from above" (James 1:17a). Joy comes from the depths of our hearts when we understand the Father's love. Praise continually comes from our lips, and we continue to point others towards Him.

The secret to joy is love. God created us with love and joy. The source of our joy is His love. His love is His Son. When we have His Son, whom He freely gave to us in love, we have joy!

The LORD has done great things for us,
and we are filled with joy
(Psalm 126:3 NIV).

Deep Roots Reflection
New Testament Word: *nahar* (Greek)
to shine, beam, light, burn, to flow[6]

This little light of mine, I'm gonna let it shine! When the Light of Christ lives in you, He can't help but shine! May He fill you so that others see Him in you and be drawn to the Light for the eternal harvest!

The secret to joy is love.

Look up the following verses and write them in the spaces provided. Then take time to answer the following questions.

Psalm 34:5 ~

____

____

____

____

If Christ shines through me, there is no room for shame. How does this affect your perspective on your life today?

____

____

____

Daniel 12:3 ~

____

____

____

*Only after the fruit has been hard-pressed
can it shine.*

How has Daniel 12:3 been revealed in your life?

____

____

____

How may it be revealed from this point forward?

____

____

____

I was like the woman at the well. God knew every detail of my life, and He met me in His perfect place in His perfect timing. My soul was thirsty. It was longing for something more. He found me and my soul found Him.

The soul is never satisfied until it meets the Savior.

Just like the roots, we flourish beside streams of living water. Healing, freedom, and nourishment are found in the river of God. We are made new and meant to thrive, so that we may produce fruit.

Our life will contain struggles and at times it may seem difficult. Press on and trust that God is at work in your life. *Only after the fruit has been hard-pressed can it shine.* "I am the vine; you are the branches. If you remain in me and I in you, you will bear much fruit; apart from me you can do nothing" (John 15:5 NIV).

Can you identify where God has pruned out an aspect of your life? Can you see how it was helpful?

____

____

____

____

____

In Him, you fit in perfectly.

In Him, you are never alone.

In Him, the legacy continues.

God gives us a nourishing, fresh drink of living water. He washes us with the Word, and our hearts are full. Gratitude can't help but overflow.

We thrive.

We shine.

We leave a beautiful legacy!

Beautiful Legacy Reminder

Your story, intricately woven into the greatest story, began at creation. You were created by God for God. You are beloved and called for a purpose, which includes sharing His love with the people He has placed in your life. Your curiosity will draw you closer to God and give you wisdom to know Him more so that His light may shine through you brilliantly. He has redeemed you, and planted the imperishable seed in your heart so you may radiate the depth of His love onto everyone you meet. Jesus is the imperishable seed and the source of true eternal beauty. The moment you believed, you were grafted into the faith-family tree, adopted as God's child, and given a Spiritual DNA. Your roots are heavenly and they run deep. May you pass this beautiful legacy on to your children, and may you bring God naches.

*For what is our hope,
our joy, or the crown
in which we will glory
in the presence of
our Lord Jesus
when he comes?
Is it not you?*

~ (1 Thessalonians 2:19 NIV).

ABOUT THE AUTHOR

 **Mindy Lee Hopman** is a Jewish believer, Bible teacher and dynamic speaker with a master's degree in Religion from Liberty University with an emphasis in Christian leadership. She also holds a master's degree in Education with an emphasis in Curriculum and Instruction from George Mason University.

Mindy's focus is on teaching believers how each person's individual faith story fits into the greatest story from the beginning to the end of time. Her grandfather was a great influence on her faith as a child, and even more so as an adult when Mindy began to understand how her Christian faith directly connected to her Jewish roots.

Mindy loves living in the comfort of the South and is a dedicated wife, mother to Hunter and Haylee, and teacher. She serves in a private day/boarding school with her husband, Jon, coaches the women group leaders in her church, and leads a prolific Bible study for women.

In her free time, Mindy loves to be with her family on the water and take sunrise and sunset pictures. You can find the pictures attached to Mindy's devotionals at **www.mindyhopman.com**.

To share how God used *Beautiful Legacy: Our Roots Run Deep* to impact your life, or to request a speaking engagement, please email Mindy at **mindyhopman@gmail.com**, or you may write to her:

Mindy Hopman
c/o Basking in His Light
P.O. Box 5172
Hilton Head Island, SC 29938

Preface: My Hope
1   Augustine, Saint, Of Hippo. Ten Homilies on the First Epistle of John, Ninth Homily. Translated by J. H. Meyers and H. Brown. 1995.
2   "History » Howard Thurman Center for Common Ground | Boston University." Howard Thurman Center for Common Ground RSS. Accessed July 07, 2016. https://www.bu.edu/thurman/about/history/.

Introduction: Naches
1   Trisha LaNae'. "A Conversation with Dr. Maya Angelou…." Beautifully Said Magazine. Accessed August 03, 2016. http://beautifullysmagazine.com/.

Chapter One: Created
1   Lewis, C. S. *Mere Christianity: Comprising The Case for Christianity, Christian Behaviour, and Beyond Personality.* New York: Touchstone, 1996, pg. 175.
2   2 Kings 2:11
3   Murray, Andrew. *The Practice of God's Presence: Humility in the Teaching of Jesus.* Pennsylvania: Whitaker House, 1982, pg. 403.
4   Ibid, pg. 132.
5   "Creating Space for God - Henri Nouwen Society." Henri Nouwen Society. Accessed June 10, 2016. http://henrinouwen.org/meditation/creating-space-god/.
6   "Dictionary.com - The World's Favorite Online Dictionary!" Dictionary.com. Accessed June/July, 2016. http://www.dictionary.com/.
7   "Genesis Chapter 1 (NASB)." Blue Letter Bible. Accessed June/July, 2016. https://www.blueletterbible.org/lang/lexicon/lexicon.cfm?t=nkjv&strongs=h1254.

Chapter Two: Beloved
1   Tileston, Mary Wilder. *Joy and Strength.* World Wide Publications. 1986, pg. 76.
2   "BibleGateway." Verses 21–25. Accessed June/July, 2016. https://www.biblegateway.com/resources/matthew-henry/Gen.2.21-Gen.2.25.
3   Murray, Andrew. *The Practice of God's Presence: Humility in the Teaching of Jesus.* Pennsylvania: Whitaker House, 1982, pg. 469.
4   "Genesis Chapter 1 (NLT)." Blue Letter Bible. Accessed July 01, 2016. https://www.blueletterbible.org/lang/lexicon/lexicon.cfm?Strongs=G319&t=NLT.
5   Poulain, Aug, and J. V. Bainvel. *The Graces of Interior Prayer: (Des Grâces D'oraison): A Treatise on Mystical Theology.* London: Routledge & Kegan Paul, 1950.
6   Christy Nockels & Nathan Nockels. *For Your Splendor.* CMG, 2012, CD. CMG LICENSE NO: 584416
7   "Genesis Chapter 1 (NASB)." Blue Letter Bible. Accessed June/July, 2016. https://www.blueletterbible.org/lang/lexicon/lexicon.cfm?t=nkjv&strongs=h2617.
8   Elliot, Elisabeth. *Keep a Quiet Heart.* Revell, Grand Rapids, 1995, pg. 156.
9   From a conference on St. Thomas Aquinas (*Opuscula*, In duo praecenta… Ed. J.P. Torrel, in Revue des Sc. Phil. Et Théol., 69, 1985, pp. 26-29) prepared by Pontifical University Urbaniana, with the collaboration of the Missionary Institutes.

Chapter Three: Curious
1   Tozer, A. W., and Edythe Draper. *The Pursuit of God.* Camp Hill, PA: Christian Publications, 1995, Pg. 141.
2   "Genesis Chapter 1 (KJV)." Blue Letter Bible. Accessed July 01, 2016. https://www.blueletterbible.org/lang/lexicon/lexicon.cfm?Strongs=G3811&t=KJV.
3   Ortberg, John. *Soul Keeping: Caring for the Most Important Part of You.* Michigan: Zondervan, 2014, Pg. 67.
4   "Christ the Conqueror of Satan." *The Spurgeon Archive.* N.p., n.d. Web. 13 July 2015.
5   Ibid.
6   "The Promised Seed: The Source of Blessing in God's Perfect Plan" Bible.org. N.p., n.d. Web. 13 July 2015.

7   Anderson, Neil T. *The Bondage Breaker*. Eugene, Or.: Harvest House, 1990. Print.

8   Ortberg, John. *Soul Keeping: Caring for the Most Important Part of You*. Michigan: Zondervan, 2014, Pg. 147.

9   Wright, Christopher J. H. *Knowing Jesus through the Old Testament*. Downers Grove, IL: InterVarsity, 1995. Print.

10 "Genesis Chapter 1 (NASB)." Blue Letter Bible. Accessed June/July, 2016. https://www.blueletterbible.org/lang/lexicon/lexicon.cfm?t=nkjv&strongs=h2233.

Chapter Four: Brilliant

1   Mills, J. S. *A Manual of Family Worship: With an Essay on the Christian Family (Classic Reprint)*. Forgotten Books, 2015, Pg. 479.

2   "Genesis Chapter 1 (NASB)." Blue Letter Bible. Accessed June/July, 2016. https://www.blueletterbible.org/lang/lexicon/lexicon.cfm?t=nkjv&strongs=h1285.

Chapter Five: Intimate

1   Murray, Andrew. *The Practice of God's Presence: The Power of the Blood of Jesus*. Pennsylvania: Whitaker House, 1993, Pg. 63-64.

2   "Genesis Chapter 1 (NASB)." Blue Letter Bible. Accessed July 30, 2016. https://www.blueletterbible.org/lang/lexicon/lexicon.cfm?Strongs=H3045&t=NASB.

3   Frankl, Viktor E. *Man's Search for Meaning*. Boston: Beacon Press, 2006, Pg. 80.

4   Ibid, Pg.115.

5   Murray, Andrew. *The Practice of God's Presence: Cleansed by the Blood to Serve the Living God*. Pennsylvania: Whitaker House, 1999, Pgs. 63-64.

6   Ortberg, John. *Soul Keeping: Caring for the Most Important Part of You*. Michigan: Zondervan, 2014, Pg. 67.

7   Voskamp, Ann. *One Thousand Gifts: A Dare to Live Fully Right Where You Are*. Grand Rapids, MI: Zondervan, 2010, Pg. 118.

8   Gower, Ralph, and Fred Wight. *The New Manners and Customs of Bible Times*. Chicago: Moody, 2004, Pg. 106.

9   "Genesis Chapter 1 (NASB)." Blue Letter Bible. Accessed June/July, 2016. https://www.blueletterbible.org/lang/lexicon/lexicon.cfm?t=nkjv&strongs=h3045.

10 Ortberg, John. *Soul Keeping: Caring for the Most Important Part of You*. Michigan: Zondervan, 2014, Pg. 89.

Chapter Six: Redeemed

1   "The Heart of the Gospel." Accessed July 01, 2016. http://biblehub.com/sermons/auth/spurgeon/the_heart_of_the_gospel.htm.

2   Tozer, A. W. *Preparing for Jesus Return: Daily Living the Blessed Hope*. Ventura: Regal, 2012, Pg. 111.

3   "Genesis Chapter 1 (NASB)." Blue Letter Bible. Accessed June/July, 2016. https://www.blueletterbible.org/lang/lexicon/lexicon.cfm?t=nkjv&strongs=h1350.

Chapter Seven: Grateful

1   Moore, Beth. *A Woman and Her God*. Brentwood: Integrity Publishers, 2003.

2   Tozer, A. W. *Preparing for Jesus Return: Daily Living the Blessed Hope*. Ventura: Regal, 2012, Pg. 88.

3   Gower, Ralph, and Fred Wight. *The New Manners and Customs of Bible Times*. Chicago: Moody, 2004, pg. 106.

4   Ibid, pg. 110.

5   "William Carey Preached Deathless Sermon." Christianity.com. Accessed July 01, 2016. http://www.christianity.com/church/church-history/timeline/1701-1800/william-carey-preached-deathless-sermon-11630317.html.

6   "Genesis Chapter 1 (NASB)." Blue Letter Bible. Accessed June/July, 2016. https://www.blueletterbible.org/lang/lexicon/lexicon.cfm?t=nkjv&strongs=g5102.